ANTIPODES

Stories by

David Malouf

Penguin Books

Penguin Books Ltd, Harmondsworth, Middlesex, England
Viking Penguin Inc., 40 West 23rd Street, New York, New York 10010, U.S.A.
Penguin Books Australia Ltd, Ringwood, Victoria, Australia
Penguin Books Canada Ltd, 2801 John Street, Markham, Ontario, Canada L3R 1B4
Penguin Books (N.Z.) Ltd, 182–190 Wairau Road, Auckland 10, New Zealand

First published by Chatto & Windus . The Hogarth Press 1985
Published in Penguin Books 1986

Printed and bound in Great Britain by
Cox & Wyman Ltd, Reading

PENGUIN BOOKS

ANTIPODES

David Malouf was born in Brisbane. His father's family came to Australia in the 1880s from Lebanon and his mother's family from London just before the First World War. He was educated at the Brisbane Grammar School and the University of Queensland, where he taught for two years after completing a degree. At the age of twenty-four he left Australia and remained abroad for nearly ten years, teaching in England and travelling in Europe. In 1968 he returned to Australia, and was appointed senior tutor and later lecturer at Sydney University. He now lives in Italy.

In 1978 he gave up teaching to write full time and one of his early major projects was to write the libretto for Patrick White's *Voss*, an opera commissioned by the Australian Opera. In 1979 he received the New South Wales Premier's Literary Award for his novel *An Imaginary Life*, and in the 1982 *Age* Australian Book of the Year Awards, *Fly Away Peter* won the Fiction award and *Child's Play* was highly commended. The last two together with his other novels, *Johnno* and *Harland's Half Acre*, are also published in Penguins. He is also well known as a poet, and his collection *Neighbours in a Thicket* won the Grace Leven Prize for Poetry, the Gold Medal of the Australian Literature Society (which he received again in 1983 for *Fly Away Peter*) and the James Cook Award for the best Australian book of 1974.

Contents

To
Judith Rodriguez and Thomas W. Shapcott

SOUTHERN SKIES

From the beginning he was a stumbling-block, the Professor. I had always thought of him as an old man, as one thinks of one's parents as old, but he can't in those days have been more than fifty. Squat, powerful, with a good deal of black hair on his wrists, he was what was called a 'ladies man' – though that must have been far in the past and in another country. What he practised now was a formal courtliness, a clicking of heels and kissing of plump fingers that was the extreme form of a set of manners that our parents clung to because it belonged, along with much else, to the Old Country, and which we young people, for the same reason, found it imperative to reject. The Professor had a 'position' – he taught mathematics to apprentices on day-release. He was proof that a breakthrough into the new world was not only possible, it was a fact. Our parents, having come to a place where their qualifications in medicine or law were unacceptable, had been forced to take work as labourers or factory-hands or to keep dingy shops; but we, their clever sons and daughters, would find our way back to the safe professional classes. For our parents there was deep sorrow in all this, and the Professor offered hope. We were invited to see in him both the embodiment of a noble past and a glimpse of what, with hard work and a little luck or grace, we might claim from the future.

He was always the special guest.

'Here, pass the Professor this slice of Torte,' my mother would say, choosing the largest piece and piling it with cream, or 'Here, take the Professor a nice cold Pils, and see you hand it to him proper now and don't spill none on the way': this on one of those community outings we used to go to in the early years, when half a dozen families would gather at Suttons Beach with a crate of beer bottles in straw jackets and a spread of homemade sausage and cabbage rolls. Aged six or seven, in my knitted bathing-briefs, and watching out in my bare feet for bindy-eye, I would set out over the grass to where the great man and my father, easy now in shirtsleeves and braces, would be pursuing one of their interminable arguments. My father had been a lawyer in the Old Country but worked now at the Vulcan Can Factory. He was passionately interested in philosophy, and the Professor was his only companion on those breathless flights that were, along with the music of Beethoven and Mahler, his sole consolation on the raw and desolate shore where he was marooned. Seeing me come wobbling towards them with the Pils – which I had slopped a little – held breast-high before me, all golden in the sun, he would look startled, as if I were a spirit of the place he had failed to allow for. It was the Professor who recognized the nature of my errand. 'Ah, how kind,' he would say. 'Thank you, my dear. And thank the good mama too. Anton, you are a lucky man.' And my father, reconciled to the earth again, would smile and lay his hand very gently on the nape of my neck while I blushed and squirmed.

The Professor had no family – or not in Australia. He lived alone in a house he had built to his own design. It was of pinewood, as in the Old Country, and in defiance of local custom was surrounded by trees – natives. There was also a swimming pool where he exercised twice a day. I went there occasionally with my father, to collect him for an outing, and had sometimes peered at it through a glass door; but we were never formally invited. The bachelor did not entertain. He was always the guest, and what his visits meant to me, as to the children of a dozen other families, was that I must be especially careful of my manners, see that my shoes were properly polished, my nails clean, my hair combed, my tie straight, my socks pulled up, and that when questioned about school or about the games I played I should give my answers clearly, precisely, and without making faces.

So there he was all through my childhood, an intimidating

presence, and a heavy reminder of that previous world; where his family owned a castle, and where he had been, my mother insisted, a real scholar.

Time passed and as the few close-knit families of our community moved to distant suburbs and lost contact with one another, we children were released from restriction. It was easy for our parents to give in to new ways now that others were not watching. Younger brothers failed to inherit our confirmation suits with their stiff white collars and cuffs. We no longer went to examinations weighed down with holy medals, or silently invoked, before putting pen to paper, the good offices of the Infant of Prague – whose influence, I decided, did not extend to Brisbane, Queensland. Only the Professor remained as a last link.

'I wish, when the Professor comes,' my mother would complain, 'that you try to speak better. The vowels! For my sake, darling, but also for your father, because we want to be proud of you,' and she would try to detain me as, barefoot, in khaki shorts and an old T-shirt, already thirteen, I wriggled from her embrace. 'And put shoes on, or sandals at least, and a nice clean shirt. I don't want that the Professor think we got an Arab for a son. And your Scout belt! And comb your hair a little, my darling – please!'

She kissed me before I could pull away. She was shocked, now that she saw me through the Professor's eyes, at how far I had grown from the little gentleman I might have been, all neatly suited and shod and brushed and polished, if they had never left the Old Country, or if she and my father had been stricter with me in this new one.

The fact is, I had succeeded, almost beyond my own expectations, in making myself indistinguishable from the roughest of my mates at school. My mother must have wondered at times if I could ever be smoothed out and civilized again, with my broad accent, my slang, my feet toughened and splayed from going barefoot. I was spoiled and wilful and ashamed of my parents. My mother knew it, and now, in front of the Professor, it was her turn to be ashamed. To assert my independence, or to show them that I did not care, I was never so loutish, I never slouched or mumbled or scowled so darkly as when the Professor appeared. Even my father, who was too dreamily involved with his own thoughts to notice me on most occasions, was aware of it and shocked. He complained to my mother, who shook her head and cried. I felt magnificently justified, and the next time the Professor made his appearance I swaggered even more outrageously and gave every indication of being an incorrigible tough.

The result was not at all what I had had in mind. Far from being repelled by my roughness the Professor seemed charmed. The more I showed off and embarrassed my parents, the more he encouraged me. My excesses delighted him. He was entranced.

He really was, as we younger people had always thought, a caricature of a man. You could barely look at him without laughing, and we had all become expert, even the girls, at imitating his hunched stance, his accent (which was at once terribly foreign and terribly English) and the way he held his stubby fingers when, at the end of a meal, he dipped sweet biscuits into wine and popped them whole into his mouth. My own imitations were designed to torment my mother.

'Oh you shouldn't!' she would whine, suppressing another explosion of giggles. 'You mustn't! Oh stop it now, your father will see – he would be offended. The Professor is a fine man. May you have such a head on your shoulders one day, and such a position.'

'Such a head on my shoulders,' I mimicked, hunching my back like a stork so that I had no neck, and she would try to cuff me, and miss as I ducked away.

I was fifteen and beginning to spring up out of pudgy childhood into clean-limbed, tumultuous adolescence. By staring for long hours into mirrors behind locked doors, by taking stock of myself in shop windows, and from the looks of some of the girls at school, I had discovered that I wasn't at all bad-looking, might even be good-looking, and was already tall and well-made. I had chestnut hair like my mother and my skin didn't freckle in the sun but turned heavy gold. There was a whole year between fifteen and sixteen when I was fascinated by the image of myself I could get back from people simply by playing up to them – it scarcely mattered whom:

teachers, girls, visitors to the house like the Professor, passers-by in the street. I was obsessed with myself, and lost no opportunity of putting my powers to the test.

Once or twice in earlier days, when I was playing football on Saturday afternoon, my father and the Professor had appeared on the sidelines, looking in after a walk. Now, as if by accident, the Professor came alone. When I came trotting in to collect my bike, dishevelled, still spattered and streaked from the game, he would be waiting. He just happened, yet again, to be passing, and had a book for me to take home, or a message: he would be calling for my father at eight and could I please remind him, or yes, he would be coming next night to play Solo. He was very formal on these occasions, but I felt his interest; and sometimes, without thinking of anything more than the warm sense of myself it gave me to command his attention, I would walk part of the way home with him, wheeling my bike and chatting about nothing very important: the game, or what I had done with my holiday, or since he was a dedicated star-gazer, the new comet that had appeared. As these meetings increased I got to be more familiar with him. Sometimes, when two or three of the others were there (they had come to recognize him and teased me a little, making faces and jerking their heads as he made his way, hunched and short-sighted, to where we were towelling ourselves at the tap) I would for their benefit show off a little, without at first realizing, in my reckless passion to be admired, that I was exceeding all bounds and that they now included me as well as the Professor in their humorous contempt. I was mortified. To ease myself back into their good opinion I passed him off as a family nuisance, whose attentions I knew were comic but whom I was leading on for my own amusement. This was acceptable enough and I was soon restored to popularity, but felt doubly treacherous. He was, after all, my father's closest friend, and there was as well that larger question of the Old Country. I burned with shame, but was too cowardly to do more than brazen things out.

For all my crudeness and arrogance I had a great desire to act nobly, and in this business of the Professor I had miserably failed. I decided to cut my losses. As soon as he appeared now, and had announced his message, I would mount my bike, sling my football boots over my shoulder and pedal away. My one fear was that he might enquire what the trouble was, but of course he did not. Instead he broke off his visits altogether or passed the field without stopping, and I found myself regretting something I had come to depend on – his familiar figure hunched like a bird on the sidelines, our talks, some fuller sense of my own presence to add at the end of the game to the immediacy of my limbs after violent exercise.

Looking back on those days I see myself as a kind of centaur, half-boy, half-bike, forever wheeling down suburban streets under the poincianas, on my way to football practice or the library or to a meeting of the little group of us, boys and girls, that came together on someone's verandah in the evenings after tea.

I might come across the Professor then on his after-dinner stroll, and as often as not he would be accompanied by my father, who would stop me and demand (partly, I thought, to impress the Professor) where I was off to or where I had been; insisting, with more than his usual force, that I come home right away, with no argument.

On other occasions, pedalling past his house among the trees, I would catch a glimpse of him with his telescope on the roof. He might raise a hand and wave if he recognized me; and sprinting away, crouched low over the handlebars, I would feel, or imagine I felt, that the telescope had been lowered and was following me to the end of the street, losing me for a time, then picking me up again two streets further on as I flashed away under the bunchy leaves.

I spent long hours cycling back and forth between our house and my girlfriend Helen's or to Ross McDowell or Jimmy Larwood's, my friends from school, and the Professor's house was always on the route.

I think of those days now as being all alike, and the nights also: the days warmish, still, endlessly without event, and the nights quivering with expectancy but also uneventful, heavy with the scent of jasmine and honeysuckle and lighted by enormous stars. But what I am describing, of course, is neither a time nor a place but the mood of my own bored, expectant, uneventful adolescence. I was always abroad and waiting for something significant to occur, for life somehow to declare itself and catch me up. I rode my bike in slow circles or figures-of-eight, took it for sprints across the gravel of the park, or simply hung motionless in the saddle, balanced and waiting.

Nothing ever happened. In the dark of front verandahs we lounged and swapped stories, heard gossip, told jokes, or played show-poker and smoked. One night each week I went to Helen's and we sat a little scared of one other in her garden-swing, touching in the dark. Helen liked me better, I thought, than I liked her – I had that power over her – and it was this more than anything else that attracted me, though I found it scary as well. For fear of losing me she might have gone to any one of the numbers that in those days marked the stages of sexual progress and could be boasted about, in a way that seemed shameful afterwards, in locker-rooms or round the edge of the pool. I could have taken us both to 6, 8, 10, but what then? The numbers were not infinite.

I rode around watching my shadow flare off gravel; sprinted, hung motionless, took the rush of warm air into my shirt; afraid that when the declaration came, it too, like the numbers, might be less than infinite. I didn't want to discover the limits of the world. Restlessly impelled towards some future that would at last offer me my real self, I nevertheless drew back, happy for the moment, even in my unhappiness, to be half-boy, half-bike, half aimless energy and half a machine that could hurtle off at a moment's notice in any one of a hundred directions. Away from things – but away, most of all, from my self. My own presence had begun to be a source of deep dissatisfaction to me, my vanity, my charm, my falseness, my preoccupation with sex. I was sick of myself and longed for the world to free me by making its own rigorous demands and declaring at last what I must be.

One night, in our warm late winter, I was riding home past the Professor's house when I saw him hunched as usual beside his telescope, but too absorbed on this occasion to be aware of me.

I paused at the end of the drive, wondering what it was that he saw on clear nights like this, that was invisible to me when I leaned my head back and filled my gaze with the sky.

The stars seemed palpably close. In the high September blueness it was as if the odour of jasmine blossoms had gathered there in a single shower of white. You might have been able to catch the essence of it floating down, as sailors, they say, can smell new land whole days before they first catch sight of it.

What I was catching, in fact, was the first breath of change – a change of season. From the heights I fell suddenly into deep depression, one of those sweet-sad glooms of adolescence that are like a bodiless drifting out of yourself into the immensity of things, when you are aware as never again – or never so poignantly – that time is moving swiftly on, that a school year is very nearly over and childhood finished, that you will have to move up a grade at football into a tougher class – shifts that against the vastness of space are minute, insignificant, but at that age solemnly felt.

I was standing astride the bike, staring upwards, when I became aware that my name was being called, and for the second or third time. I turned my bike into the drive with its border of big-leafed saxifrage and came to where the Professor, his hand on the telescope, was leaning out over the roof.

'I have some books for your father,' he called. 'Just come to the gate and I will get them for you.'

The gate was wooden, and the fence, which made me think of a stockade, was of raw slabs eight feet high, stained reddish-brown. He leaned over the low parapet and dropped a set of keys.

'It's the thin one,' he told me. 'You can leave your bike in the yard.' He meant the paved courtyard inside, where I rested it easily against the wall. Beyond, and to the left of the pine-framed house, which was stained the same colour as the fence, was a garden taken up almost entirely by the pool. It was overgrown with dark tropical plants, monstera, hibiscus, banana-palms with their big purplish flowers, glossily pendulous on stalks, and fixed to the paling-fence like trophies in wads of bark, elk-horn, tree-orchids, showers of delicate maidenhair. It was too cold for swimming, but the pool was filled and covered with a shifting scum of jacaranda leaves that had blown in from the street, where the big trees were stripping to bloom.

I went round the edge of the pool and a light came on, reddish, in one of the inner rooms. A moment later the Professor himself appeared, tapping for attention at a glass door.

'I have the books right here,' he said briskly; but when I stood hesitating in the dark beyond the threshold, he shifted his feet and added: 'But maybe you would like to come in a moment and have a drink. Coffee. I could make some. Or beer. Or a Coke if you prefer it. I have Coke.'

I had never been here alone, and never, even with my father, to this side of the house. When we came to collect the Professor for an outing we had always waited in the tiled hallway while he rushed about with one arm in the sleeve of his overcoat laying out saucers for cats, and it was to the front door, in later years, that I had delivered bowls of gingerbread fish that my mother had made specially because she knew he liked it, or cabbage rolls or herring. I had never been much interested in what lay beyond the hallway, with its fierce New Guinea masks, all tufted hair and boar's tusks, and the Old Country chest that was just like our own. Now, with the books already in my hands, I hesitated and looked past him into the room.

'All right. If it's no trouble.'

'No no, no trouble at all!' He grinned, showing his teeth with their extravagant caps. 'I am delighted. Really! Just leave the books there. You see they are tied with string, quite easy for you I'm sure, even on the bike. Sit where you like. Anywhere. I'll get the drink.'

'Beer then,' I said boldly, and my voice cracked, destroying what I had hoped might be the setting of our relationship on a clear, man-to-man basis that would wipe out the follies of the previous year. I coughed, cleared my throat, and said again 'Beer, thanks,' and sat abruptly on a sofa that was too low and left me prone and sprawling.

He stopped a moment and considered, as if I had surprised him by crossing a second threshold.

'Well then, if it's to be beer, I shall join you. Maybe you are also hungry. I could make a sandwich.'

'No, no thank you, they're expecting me. Just the beer.'

He went out, his slippers shushing over the tiles, and I shifted immediately to a straight-backed chair opposite and took the opportunity to look around.

There were rugs on the floor, old threadbare Persians, and low down, all round the walls, stacks of the heavy seventy-eights I carried home when my father borrowed them: sonatas by Beethoven, symphonies by Sibelius and Mahler. Made easy by the Professor's absence, I got up and wandered round. On every open surface, the glass table-top, the sideboard, the long mantel of the fireplace, were odd bits and pieces that he must have collected in his travels: lumps of coloured quartz, a desert rose, slabs of clay with fern or fish fossils in them, glass paperweights, snuff-boxes, meerschaum pipes of fantastic shape – one a Saracen's head, another the torso of a woman like a ship's figurehead with full breasts and golden nipples – bits of Baltic amber, decorated sherds of pottery, black on terra-cotta, and one unbroken object, a little earthenware lamp that when I examined it more closely turned out to be a phallic grotesque. I had just discovered what it actually was when the Professor stepped into the room. Turning swiftly to a framed photograph on the wall above, I found myself peering into a stretch of the Old Country, a foggy, sepia world that I recognized immediately from similar photographs at home.

'Ah,' he said, setting the tray down on an empty chair, 'you have discovered my weakness.' He switched on another lamp. 'I have tried, but I am too sentimental. I cannot part with them.'

The photograph, I now observed, was one of three. They were all discoloured with foxing on the passe-partout mounts, and the glass of one was shattered, but so neatly that not a single splinter had shifted in the frame.

The one I was staring at was of half a dozen young men in military uniform. It might have been from the last century, but there was a date in copperplate: 1921. Splendidly booted and sashed and frogged, and hieratically stiff, with casque helmets under their arms, swords tilted at the thigh, white gloves tucked into braided epaulettes, they were a chorus line from a Ruritanian operetta. They were also, as I knew, the heroes of a lost but unforgotten war.

'You recognize me?' the Professor asked.

I looked again. It was difficult. All the young men strained upright with the same martial hauteur, wore the same little clipped moustaches, had the same flat hair parted in the middle and combed in wings over their ears. Figures from the past can be as foreign, as difficult to identify individually, as the members of another race. I took the plunge, set my forefinger against the frame, and turned to the Professor for confirmation. He came to my side and peered.

'No,' he said sorrowfully. 'But the mistake is entirely understandable. He was my great friend, almost a brother. I am here. This is me. On the left.'

He considered himself, the slim assured figure, chin slightly tilted, eyes fixed ahead, looking squarely out of a class whose privileges – inherent in every point of the stance, the uniform, the polished accoutrements – were not to be questioned, and from the ranks of an army that was invincible. The proud caste no longer existed. Neither did the army nor the country it was meant to defend, except in the memory of people like the Professor and my parents and, in a ghostly way, half a century off in another hemisphere, my own.

He shook his head and made a clucking sound. 'Well,' he said firmly, 'it's a long time ago. It is foolish of me to keep such things. We should live for the present. Or like you younger people', bringing the conversation back to me, 'for the future.'

I found it easier to pass to the other photographs.

In one, the unsmiling officer appeared as an even younger man, caught in an informal, carefully posed moment with a group of ladies. He was clean-shaven and lounging on the grass in a striped blazer; beside him a discarded boater – very English. The ladies, more decorously disposed, wore long dresses with hats and ribbons. Neat little slippers peeped out under their skirts.

'Yes, yes,' he muttered, almost impatient now, 'that too. Summer holidays – who can remember where? And the other a walking trip.'

I looked deep into a high meadow, with broken cloud-drift in the dip below. Three young men in shorts, maybe schoolboys, were climbing on the far side of the wars. There were flowers in the foreground, glowingly out of focus, and it was this picture whose glass was shattered; it was like looking through a brilliant spider's web into a picturebook landscape that was utterly familiar, though I could never have been there. *That is the place,* I thought. *That is the land my parents mean when they say 'the Old Country': the country of childhood and first love that they go back to in their sleep and which I have no memory of, though I was born there. Those flowers are the ones, precisely those, that blossom in the songs they sing.* And immediately I was back in my mood of just a few minutes ago, when I had stood out there gazing up at the stars. *What is it,* I asked myself, *that I will remember and want to preserve, when in years to come I think of the Past? What will be important enough?* For what the photographs had led me back to, once again, was myself. It was always the same. No matter how hard I tried to think my way out into other people's lives, into the world beyond me, the feelings I discovered were my own.

'Come. Sit,' the Professor said, 'and drink your beer. And do eat one of these sandwiches. It's very good rye bread, from the only shop. I go all the way to South Brisbane for it. And Gürken. I seem to remember you like them.'

'What do you do up on the roof?' I asked, my mouth full of bread and beer, feeling uneasy again now that we were sitting with nothing to fix on.

'I make observations, you know. The sky, which looks so still, is always in motion, full of drama if you understand how to read it. Like looking into a pond. Hundreds of events happening right under your eyes, except that most of what we see is already finished by the time we see it – ages ago – but important just the same. Such large events. Huge! Bigger even than we can imagine. And beautiful, since they unfold, you know, to a kind of music, to numbers of infinite dimension like the ones you deal with in equations at school, but more complex, and entirely visible.'

He was moved as he spoke by an emotion that I could not identify, touched by occasions a million light-years off and still unfolding towards him, in no way personal. The room for a moment lost its tension. I no longer felt myself to be the focus of his interest, or even of my own. I felt liberated, and for the first time the Professor was interesting in his own right, quite apart from the attention he paid me or the importance my parents attached to him.

'Maybe I could come again,' I found myself saying. 'I'd like to see.'

'But of course,' he said, 'any time. Tonight is not good – there is a little haze, but tomorrow if you like. Or any time.'

I nodded. But the moment of easiness had passed. My suggestion, which might have seemed like another move in a game, had brought me back into focus for him and his look was quizzical, defensive. I felt it and was embarrassed, and at the same time saddened. Some truer vision of myself had been in the room for a moment. I had almost grasped it. Now I felt it slipping away as I moved back into my purely physical self.

I put the glass down, not quite empty.

'No thanks, really,' I told him when he indicated the half finished bottle on the tray. 'I should have been home nearly an hour ago. My mother, you know.'

'Ah yes, of course. Well, just call whenever you wish, no need to be formal. Most nights I am observing. It is a very interesting time. Here – let me open the door for you. The books, I see, are a little awkward, but you are so expert on the bicycle I am sure it will be OK.'

I followed him round the side of the pool into the courtyard and there was my bike at its easy angle to the wall, my other familiar and streamlined self. I wheeled it out while he held the gate.

Among my parents' oldest friends were a couple who had recently moved to a new house on the other side of the park, and at the end of winter, in the year I turned seventeen, I sometimes rode over on Sundays to help John clear the big overgrown garden. All afternoon we grubbed out citrus trees that had gone wild, hacked down morning-glory that had grown all over the lower part of the yard, and cut the knee-high grass with a sickle to prepare it for mowing.

I enjoyed the work. Stripped down to shorts in the strong sunlight, I slashed and tore at the weeds till my hands blistered, and in a trancelike preoccupation with tough green things that clung to the earth with a fierce tenacity, forgot for a time my own turmoil and lack of roots. It was something to *do*.

John, who worked up ahead, was a dentist. He paid me ten shillings a day for the work, and this, along with my pocket-money, would take Helen and me to the pictures on Saturday night, or to a flash meal at one of the city hotels. We worked all afternoon, while the children, who were four and seven, watched and got in the way. Then about five-thirty Mary would call us for tea.

Mary had been at school with my mother and was the same age, though I could never quite believe it; she had children a whole ten years younger than I was, and I had always called her Mary. She wore bright bangles on her arm, liked to dance at parties, never gave me presents like handkerchiefs or socks, and had always treated me, I thought, as a grown-up. When she called us for tea I went to the garden tap, washed my feet, splashed water over my back that was streaked with soil and sweat and stuck all over with little grass clippings, and was about to buckle on my loose sandals when she said from the doorway where she had been watching: 'Don't bother to get dressed. John hasn't.' She stood there smiling, and I turned away, aware suddenly of how little I had on; and had to use my V-necked sweater to cover an excitement that might otherwise have been immediately apparent in the khaki shorts I was wearing – without underpants because of the heat.

As I came up the steps towards her she stood back to let me pass, and her hand, very lightly, brushed the skin between my shoulder-blades.

'You're still wet,' she said.

It seemed odd somehow to be sitting at the table in their elegant dining-room without a shirt; though John was doing it, and was already engaged like the children in demolishing a pile of neat little sandwiches.

I sat at the head of the table with the children noisily grabbing at my left and John on my right drinking tea and slurping it a little, while Mary plied me with raisin-bread and Old Country cookies. I felt red, swollen, confused every time she turned to me, and for some reason it was the children's presence rather than John's that embarrassed me, especially the boy's.

Almost immediately we were finished John got up.

'I'll just go,' he said, 'and do another twenty minutes before it's dark.' It was dark already, but light enough perhaps to go on raking the grass we had cut and were carting to the incinerator. I made to follow. 'It's all right,' he told me. 'I'll finish off. You've earned your money for today.'

'Come and see our animals!' the children yelled, dragging me down the hall to their bedroom, and for ten minutes or so I sat on the floor with them, setting out farm animals and making fences, till Mary, who had been clearing the table, appeared in the doorway.

'Come on now, that's enough, it's bathtime, you kids. Off you go!'

They ran off, already half-stripped, leaving her to pick up their clothes and fold them while I continued to sit cross-legged among the toys, and her white legs, in their green sandals, moved back and forth at eye-level. When she went out I too got up, and stood watching at the bathroom door.

She was sitting on the edge of the bath, soaping the little boy's back, as I remembered my mother doing, while the children splashed and shouted. Then she dried her hands on a towel, very carefully, and I followed her into the unlighted lounge. Beyond the glass wall, in the depths of the garden, John was stooping to gather armfuls of the grass we had cut, and staggering with it to the incinerator.

She sat and patted the place beside her. I followed as in a dream. The children's voices at the end of the hallway were complaining, quarrelling, shrilling. I was sure John could see us through the glass as he came back for another load.

Nothing was said. Her hand moved over my shoulder, down my spine, brushed very lightly, without lingering, over the place where my shorts tented; then rested easily on my thigh. When John came in he seemed unsurprised to find us sitting close in the dark. He went right past us to the drinks cabinet, which suddenly lighted up.

I felt exposed and certain now that he must see where her hand was and say something.

All he said was: 'Something to drink, darling?'

Without hurry she got up to help him and they passed back and forth in front of the blazing cabinet, with its mirrors and its rows of bottles and cut-crystal glasses. I was sweating worse than when I had worked in the garden, and began, self-consciously, to haul on the sweater.

I pedalled furiously away, glad to have the cooling air pour over me and to feel free again.

Back there I had been scared – but of what? Of a game in which I might, for once, be the victim – not passive, but with no power to control the moves. I slowed down and considered that, and was, without realizing it, at the edge of something. I rode on in the softening dark. It was good to have the wheels of the bike roll away under me as I rose on the pedals, to feel on my cheeks the warm scent of jasmine that was invisible all round. It was a brilliant night verging on spring. I didn't want it to be over; I wanted to slow things down. I dismounted and walked a little, leading my bike along the grassy edge in the shadow of trees, and without precisely intending it, came on foot to the entrance to the Professor's drive, and paused, looking up beyond the treetops to where he might be installed with his telescope – observing what? What events up there in the infinite sky?

I leaned far back to see. A frozen waterfall it might have been, falling slowly towards me, sending out blown spray that would take centuries, light-years, to break in thunder over my head. Time. What did one moment, one night, a lifespan mean in relation to all that?

'Hullo there!'

It was the Professor. I could see him now, in the moonlight beside the telescope, which he leaned on and which pointed not upward to the heavens but down to where I was standing. It occurred to me, as on previous occasions, that in the few moments of my standing there with my head flung back to the stars, what he might have been observing was *me*. I hesitated, made no decision. Then, out of a state of passive expectancy, willing nothing but waiting poised for my own life to occur; out of a state of being open to the spring night and to the emptiness of the hours between seven and ten when I was expected to be in, or thirteen (was it?) and whatever age I would be when manhood finally came to me; out of my simply being there with my hand on the saddle of the machine, bare-legged, loose-sandalled, going nowhere, I turned into the drive, led my bike up to the stockade gate and waited for him to throw down the keys.

'You know which one it is,' he said, letting them fall. 'Just use the other to come in by the poolside.'

I unlocked the gate, rested my bike against the wall of the courtyard and went round along the edge of the pool. It was clean now but heavy with shadows. I turned the key in the glass door, found my way (though this part of the house was new to me) to the stairs, and climbed to where another door opened straight on to the roof.

'Ah,' he said, smiling. 'So at last! You are here.'

The roof was unwalled but set so deep among trees that it was as if I had stepped out of the city altogether into some earlier, more darkly-wooded era. Only lighted windows, hanging detached in the dark, showed where houses, where neighbours were.

He fixed the telescope for me and I moved into position. 'There,' he said, 'what you can see now is Jupiter with its four moons – you see? – all in line, and with the bands across its face.'

I saw. Later it was Saturn with its rings and the lower of the two pointers to the cross, Alpha Centauri, which was not one star but two. It was miraculous. From that moment below when I had looked up at a cascade of light that was still ages off, I might have been catapulted twenty thousand years into the nearer past, or into my own future. Solid spheres hovered above me, tiny balls of matter moving in concert like the atoms we drew in chemistry, held together by invisible lines of force; and I thought oddly that if I were to lower the telescope now to where I had been standing at the entrance to the drive I would see my own puzzled, upturned face, but as a self I had already outgrown and abandoned, not minutes but aeons back. He shifted the telescope and I caught my breath. One after another, constellations I had known since childhood as points of light to be joined up in the mind (like those picture-puzzles children make, pencilling in the scattered dots till Snow White and the Seven Dwarfs appear, or an old jalopy), came together now, not as an imaginary panhandle or bull's head or belt and sword, but at some depth of vision I hadn't known I possessed, as blossoming abstractions, equations luminously exploding out of their own depths, brilliantly solving themselves and playing the results in my head as a real and visible music. I felt a power in myself that might actually burst out at my ears, and at the same time saw myself, from *out there,* as just a figure with his eye to a lens. I had a clear sense of being one more hard little point in the immensity – but part of it, a source of light like all those others – and was aware for the first time of the grainy reality of my own life, and then, a fact of no large significance, of the certainty of my death; but in some dimension where those terms were too vague to be relevant. It was at the point where my self ended and the rest of it began that Time, or Space, showed its richness to me. I was overwhelmed.

Slowly, from so far out, I drew back, re-entered the present and was aware again of the close suburban dark – of its moving now in the shape of a hand. I must have known all along that it was there, working from the small of my back to my belly, up the inside of my thigh, but it was of no importance, I was too far off. Too many larger events were unfolding for me to break away and ask, as I might have, 'What are you doing?'

I must have come immediately. But when the stars blurred in my eyes it was with tears, and it was the welling of this deeper salt, filling my eyes and rolling down my cheeks, that was the real overflow of the occasion. I raised my hand to brush them away and it was only then that I was aware, once again, of the Professor. I looked at him as from a distance. He was getting to his feet, and his babble of concern, alarm, self-pity, sentimental recrimination, was incomprehensible to me. I couldn't see what he meant.

'No no, it's nothing,' I assured him, turning aside to button my shorts. 'It was nothing. Honestly.' I was unwilling to say more in case he misunderstood what I did not understand myself.

We stood on opposite sides of the occasion. Nothing of what he had done could make the slightest difference to me, I was untouched: youth is too physical to accord very much to that side of things. But what I had *seen* – what he had led me to see – my bursting into the life of things – I would look back on that as the real beginning of my existence, as the entry into a vocation, and nothing could diminish the gratitude I felt for it. I wanted, in the immense seriousness and humility of this moment, to tell him so, but I lacked the words, and silence was fraught with all the wrong ones.

'I have to go now,' was what I said.

'Very well. Of course.'

He looked hopeless. He might have been waiting for me to strike him a blow – not a physical one. He stood quietly at the gateway while I wheeled out the bike.

I turned then and faced him, and without speaking, offered him, very formally, my hand. He took it and we shook – as if, in the magnanimity of my youth, I had agreed to overlook his misdemeanour or forgive him. That misapprehension too was a weight I would have to bear.

Carrying it with me, a heavy counterpoise to the extraordinary lightness that was my whole life, I bounced unsteadily over the dark tufts of the driveway and out onto the road.

A TRIP TO THE
GRUNDELSEE

They were an ill-assorted party.

Gordon and Cassie, who had known one another almost since childhood, were still just friends, as they had been for so long now that Cassie despaired of their ever getting further. She had spent four years being in love with Gordon and felt a fool, but was still under his spell. His various forms of selfishness, all so frank and boyishly certain of their appeal, still worked on her, and she knew that if he made the least offer of himself she would say yes and spend the rest of her life typing his articles, keeping up with his interests and defending him from detractors. That's how she was, and that's how Gordon was as well.

She had simply rushed down here, for example, the moment she thought he was involved, but by the time she arrived he had already lost interest in the girl who had turned up so frequently in his letters of the previous month, and Cassie, who had disliked Anick at sight, soon made a friend of her, seeing quite clearly that this spoiled and rather unworldly French girl would be no more successful with Gordon than she had been. She had even at last grown fond of her – they had something in common; though Anick was elegant, almost beautiful, and Cassie had never been either.

Anick made up the third in their party, and the fourth was a soft American youth of not much more than twenty who earlier in the week had fallen in love with Anick and had since been following her about like a whipped puppy. Anick tended to laugh at him, but when he cried, as he often did, she let him sit with his head in her lap while she stroked his floppy hair, but at the same time made faces; and afterwards made the same faces when she described the scene to Cassie in her limited and brutal English.

Michael, the American boy, was really Austrian – that is, his parents were, but he spoke worse German than the rest of them (they were all doing a summer course at Graz) and was foolishly impressed by everything foreign and picturesque: by the Alpine cabins they passed with their carved wooden overhangs, by votive crosses high up in the mist of passes, the leather shorts and dirndls of villagers, a little steepled church in a cleft among firs, and the pumpy band-music that was being played in one place in the light of a thunderous waterfall. Gordon and Cassie were Australians, but they had never been so wide-eyed and impressionable as Michael, to whom all this might, after all, have been as familiar as home.

Michael had hired a car and they were driving down to the Grundelsee to visit two middle-aged women who had been friends of Michael's father before the war. It was, on Michael's part, a duty visit made on his father's behalf, but also to fulfil a promise he had given, when just a child, to the elder of the two women with whom he had had a schoolboy correspondence. Gordon and Cassie were along because Anick had invited them. She hadn't wanted to spend a whole day alone with Michael. Michael resented this and they felt uncomfortable, but had accepted for the sake of the trip, though Cassie, who took on new loyalties very easily, and stuck to them, included Anick in her reasons for going; she was offering female support. She rather despised Michael and found his mooning over Anick disgusting, whereas Gordon, intent on the landscape and excited by the prospect of adding yet another baroque abbey to his list – and such a remote one – was merely indifferent.

'Another Kaisersaal!' Gordon exulted. (Being impressed by a Kaisersaal rather than a cabin made him different from Michael. Superior.) 'Another Kindertotentorte,' Cassie thought, making up with this minor disloyalty for her slavish adoption of all Gordon's vagaries of taste.

An ill-assorted party.

'What are these ladies?' Anick demanded, preparing to find them dull.

'They were my father's closest friends in Vienna before the war,' Michael told them solemnly. 'In the days of Dollfuss, you know. Elsa Fischer and my father were going to be married, I guess. The other one, Sophie, is sort of my father's cousin. They were all in the same political group. My father was a Socialist – practically even a Communist – and they spent seven years – I mean Elsa and Sophie did – in camps. You know – concentration camps. They had a really terrible time. Boy! You should hear some of the things that happened to them. But they survived. And now they live together and have this little summer place on the lake.'

Cassie was frowning. She had tried to keep up with it, to let it enter her imagination as well as her head, but Michael went too fast. His narrative made all events sound the same, and outside the sun was flashing.

'And your father?' she demanded, grabbing at a comprehensible fact.

'Oh, he escaped. He got away to America just before the Nazis came. It was a very close thing. He's told me all about it, it's a real adventure story. And of course he married my mother. But you know – he used to talk a lot about the old days, and after the war, when he and Elsa and Sophie made contact again, I used to write to Elsa – I was just a school-kid – and well – now that I'm here it's the least I can do, to go and say hello.'

The silence was filled with intensely dark fir trees, and above them the hard, unchanging whiteness of the Alps.

'They sound fascinating, these old women,' said Anick.

Michael failed to catch her tone. 'Well,' he said, after a pause, 'they're sort of special – you know what I mean?' He added a more specific recommendation: 'They've *suffered* a lot.'

It was a warm day. They had thrown their jackets aside, the two young men, and the girls were stockingless and in open sandals. They had already stopped once and eaten the most delicious cheese-cake with cream on top, heaped Schlagobers that were absolutely continuous, Gordon assured them, with the confectionary clouds of local altars. The villages they passed were all very festive-looking, with boxes of bright red geraniums in the windows and in baskets on some of the wooden bridges, and the Alps were permanently, dazzlingly white along the skyline: so that Cassie wondered why she felt so depressed.

They were all four young and their whole lives were before them.

The big car waltzed and Michael took the mountain road at speed. They hoped to be at the Grundelsee before lunch.

The lake was tiny – you could walk around it in under an hour – and glassily blue, with fir trees in dark clumps making wedge shapes and rhomboids on the slopes, and very green meadows. The summer places, scattered in groups, were all made of the same stained timber and had the same painted shutters, each with a heart cut out of it, and the same shingle roofs. A cow here and there made the scene look pastoral, productive, but bathers along the shore, and a yellow canoe out in the middle of the lake, pulling a long thread in its picture of blue mountain-peaks, certified that this was a pleasure park and that the slightly sinister atmosphere that hung over it was a matter of weather, the oppressive proximity of so much heaped sublimity.

Perfect Mahler, Gordon would have said.

What Cassie thought was: perfect Grimm.

The one piece of history the place boasted was the elopement, nearly a century before, of the post-master's daughter and an archduke. A local inn commemorated the occurrence with a painted sign. There were portraits of the couple on all the fluttering racks on the news kiosks – she young and pretty, he an old buffer with side-whiskers – and within minutes of their arrival the two ladies had first asked if they knew the story and then recited, in tandem, its romantic facts, promising to show them later the exact spot where the lovers first met and the old post-house where the girl's parents had lived. Everything had been preserved, of course, and was properly kept up. People came from all over to visit, and apart from the beauty of the views it was the postmaster's daughter, Anna

Plöhl, and the Archduke Johann who drew them. That gay fragment of not-too-recent history was what they came to savour and record.

The ladies were rather surprised by their ignorance but delighted that what they had come for was simply and entirely *them*. They hadn't been expected, of course – or not so many – but never mind, they were welcome anyway.

The more impressive of the two was definitely Elsa Fischer, a tall woman with a streak of steel-grey across her head. She was still handsome, and still preserved the assurance of what must once have been a remarkable beauty; but one felt she had long since dismissed that as a trivial gift and valued only the insights it had brought her. In learning to exploit her beauty she had learned how to deal with power; the one lasted after the other had become no more than good posture, good bones, and a little repertoire of gestures that still suggested availability – the promise of great sad occasions and moments of abandon. If she continued to play the game it was because men recognized in her a woman who knew the rules, and liked to experience, now that there was none, the sense of risk.

It was Cassie who saw all this. In her ugly-duckling way she valued beauty, had pondered the subject deeply, and was made aware of Elsa Fischer's great measure of that ambiguous gift in the effect it was having on Gordon. He had ceased to be plumply bored and was giving this sixty-year-old woman the sort of attention he reserved for churches, some paintings and everything to do with himself.

Cassie was in anguish. She wanted her life, she wanted it at all costs. But she despised the means she had to use, and had been using, to get it – the humiliations, the pretence that she had no passion, no ambition of her own, no sense of honour. Most of all she was afraid that if it came to the point she might not be willing to suffer. She writhed in a dark and stolid silence.

The other woman, who was smaller in every way than Elsa Fischer, had red hair rather inexpertly coloured, red-rimmed eyes and a drooping nose, and seemed quite incapable of being still. She had wept when Michael greeted her and clung to his neck: he was so much like his father.

'Isn't he just like Arnold?' she had said.

Elsa Fischer, who kissed him on the forehead and was not tearful, looked at him with her wide blue eyes.

'No,' she said, 'I do not see it. You already look American, Michael dear, and a good thing too. It's how you should look.' She kissed him again. 'I hoped you'd come.'

'But of course,' he began.

'No, there is no of course. But you are here, that is what matters.' And immediately, since she was aware that she had given him all the attention so far, and since there were, after all, others, she had begun to ask questions, weigh answers, demand qualifications, put things together, and soon had them all clear; and since that is what plainly offered in Gordon's awakened interest, had settled her steady gaze on *him*. Cassie watched him respond, and grow alert and painfully attractive, and oh so youthfully promising as he took out all his little talents and made them shine.

She felt one of her black clouds, the one that had been riding just above her head all morning like a bleak halo, descend at last and smother her in gloom. She felt removed. She watched from a distance. And it occurred to her that if she ever stopped being under Gordon's spell she would hate him.

Was that the cloud?

The red-headed lady, in the meantime, had gone behind a partition, and Cassie, who might have been able to see through walls, saw her, at a little shelf, put slices of meat on pumpernickel and stand there in the half-dark pushing the stuff into one side of her face; vigorously working her jaws and gulping, so that her scalp, with its shock of coloured hair, moved up and down and her throat muscles formed stringy cords. She ate one slice, then another, then a third. Cassie was mesmerized. At last, after swallowing a difficult mouthful, she composed her features, swept her hair with a light hand, and came back into the room looking dignified. She sat, and when she caught Cassie looking at her, produced a smile that was all innocence.

Elsa Fischer, who looked untouchable and gave the impression of having always been so, had been speaking in a low concerned voice of Michael Pacher, his noble forms and glowing colours, while Gordon asked questions to which, Cassie reminded herself, he already knew the answers.

The questions blunt Cassie wanted to put were these. What about the suffering? How do you know if you can face it? Do you just go through it and come out the other side? Does time dull the pain and anger of it?

'Did you see?' Anick hissed, catching up with her on the lakeside path where they were walking to a restaurant. 'She was *eating*. All by herself, behind the wall.'

'Oh, well,' said Cassie, as if there were extenuating circumstances. She hadn't Anick's clear notions of how people should and should not behave. People were extraordinary or plain odd, that was all.

'I was disgusted,' Anick declared. 'I found it insulting. Now she will come to the restaurant and say she is not 'ungree. I know such people. 'Orreeble!'

She was right. At the restaurant both ladies excused themselves and said they had already eaten, but Elsa Fischer drank a glass of wine and made recommendations and insisted they all try the local Torte. It was uncomfortable, even Gordon looked uneasy. He didn't know how he should act, and felt that some situation he had been handling very well, very urbanely, just a while back had turned into something he couldn't handle at all. Only Michael seemed untroubled. He had done the right thing already, simply by coming. He smiled incessantly and looked softly angelic. He ate heartily, drank too much, and on the walk back tried to hold Anick's hand on the narrow path, and looked hurt when she shook him off.

Cassie's cloud refused to shift. Everything gave off a kind of blackness that added to it like smoke: the food they ate, the talk, the water, the damp meadows with the shadow of firs on them, the terrible peaks. It seemed to her that the lake might contain unbearable secrets – drowned babies, or the records, deep-sunk in leaden boxes, of an era – and that these made up the weather to which her cloud belonged, and enveloped her even in sunshine in deepest gloom. It might just be that she had stepped, back there, across a border into the rest of her life and it would go on like this for the next thirty, forty, fifty years – into another century.

As they sped back down the autobahn, through fields that threw off wave after wave of heat, she sat far back in the seat with her eyes closed and let the others, all of them, sink into the dark. Their faces faded, their voices. It seemed boundless, her depression, eternally deep; though in fact, ten years later, married to another quite different Australian, and with three exuberant daughters who liked to sing in the car as she drove them to and from school, she would not recall this particular gloom, or its cause, and had lost contact with all the members of their trip but Anick, who had started up a correspondence and then kept it going long after Gordon, the original reason, had departed from their lives.

'Who *is* Anick?' the little girls would chorus as they stared at an old album, finding it difficult to connect the slim girl under the peach tree with the lady in Paris who sent them expensive, rather inappropriate presents, or the bony figure in peasant skirt and T-shirt with their comfortable mother. Something more than time seemed to be involved here.

'Anick,' Cassie would tell them, not quite sincerely, 'is mummy's best friend,' and would add, out of loyalty to one or two neighbours, 'in Europe.'

Once a year, at Christmas, the presents arrived; and then on a trip to Paris, ten years after their first encounter, Cassie made her decision and looked Anick up. They had lunch together.

Anick was still unmarried. A hard, discontented girl of thirty, still strikingly good-looking, she had that mixture of slovenliness and chic that Cassie, to whom chic would be forever foreign, thought of as uniquely French. She seemed much occupied with her digestion, eating little and accepting from the waiter, with only a nod of acknowledgement as she rattled on, the glass of mineral water she had not had to call for. It was for her medicine. Still talking, she took from her elegant bag a bottle of some thick white stuff, swallowed a spoonful, made a face that Cassie recalled from other occasions, and washed it down with a draught of Perrier and a wrathful 'Ugh'.

Thank God I don't have a digestion, Cassie thought. That'd be worse than the Black Cloud. She felt embarrassed by her bouncy good health. She was never ill – barring pregnancies of course, which didn't count.

'Cheers,' Anick proclaimed dolefully, shaking the remains of her mineral water to make it fizz. And Cassie, who felt extraordinarily liberated, shouted in response, 'Haro!', and might have done a little dance on the spot, in the manner of her youngest daughter when they were out on a hunting party being vengeful squaws. Anick looked astonished, and then delighted by what she recognized as a form of behaviour she couldn't have indulged in herself but which pleased her in others. Cassie had always, in her eyes, been marvellously free. 'Haro!' Cassie shouted again, and gave one of her deep wheezy laughs, kicking up imaginary heels and draining her half of Burgundy.

Her smile was one of triumph. What she had caught sight of – the tail-end of a darker possibility, back there, that still haunted her at times – had gone to earth, startled perhaps by the exuberance of her war cry; it needn't again, for a moment, be disturbed. And Anick, who had never even caught sight of it or known they were on a hunting party at all, looked puzzled, but did her best to enter the spirit of things, though she didn't rise to a 'Haro!'

They continued to face one another for a whole hour in the mutual perplexity of their national styles and from the vantage point of different lives, while Cassie tried to give some indication of the close web of her life as it involved three little girls, all extraordinarily different from one another and from herself, and a husband whose difficulty both challenged and pleased her. But the particulars of domesticity told nothing. They were flat, uninteresting. It was a holding warmth she needed to express, and she might have illustrated it best by simply leaning across the table and grasping Anick's neat little hand in her own larger, coarser one.

She did not. Instead she watched the details she provided in response to Anick's questions about colour of eyes and hair, the car

– a station wagon! – the number of rooms in their house, slot in under the French girl's mascara and become a dead ordinary place – 'orreebly provincial – where she had settled for a quiet, an ordinary fate.

But I am happy, she wanted to protest. I almost lost my life. And then, by the skin of my teeth, I saved it.

But there was no way of explaining this. They had no shared language, most of all when it came to the smaller words. She began to wonder, as her high spirits evaporated, what she and Anick had ever had in common.

Oh yes! She had almost forgotten. Gordon!

'No,' she said matter-of-factly. It astonished her that it was Anick, after so long, who most clearly remembered. 'I haven't seen him for years. Sydney's a big place. He's in town planning or something.'

Anick nodded.

There was nothing more to be said. Or rather, there was what there had always been. Cassie continued to write long jaunty letters in her formal, seventeenth-century French, mostly because it pleased her to tell about her children, adding more and more to Anick's image of the 'orreeble place and describing in sinister detail trips to resorts Anick would never have wanted to visit and could never find on the map. Anick continued to send postcards and presents.

The time came when this was, for each of them, their oldest and most satisfying correspondence. The children no longer asked 'Who is Anick?', not even to have the pleasure of hearing the known answer and of closing, with a rhythmic question and response, one of the gaps in their world. Instead they told their schoolfriends, rather grandly: 'This is from Anick, our mummy's best friend – in Europe.'

Europe was a place they would visit one day and see for themselves.

THE EMPTY
LUNCH-TIN

He had been there for a long time. She could not remember when she had last looked across the lawn and he was not standing in the wide, well-clipped expanse between the buddleia and the flowering quince, his shoulders sagging a little, his hands hanging limply at his side. He stood very still with his face lifted towards the house, as a tradesman waits who has rung the doorbell, received no answer, and hopes that someone will appear at last at an upper window. He did not seem in a hurry. Heavy bodies barged through the air, breaking the stillness with their angular cries. Currawongs. Others hopped about on the grass, their tails switching from side to side. Black metronomes. He seemed unaware of them. Originally the shadow of the house had been at his feet, but it had drawn back before him as the morning advanced, and he stood now in a wide sunlit space casting his own shadow. Behind him cars rushed over the warm bitumen, station-wagons in which children were being ferried to school or kindergarten, coloured delivery vans, utilities – there were no fences here; the garden was open to the street. He stood. And the only object between him and the buddleia was an iron pipe that rose two feet out of the lawn like a periscope.

At first, catching sight of him as she passed the glass wall of the dining-room, the slight figure with its foreshortened shadow, she had given a sharp little cry. Greg! And it might have been Greg standing there with only the street behind him. He would have been just that age. Doubting her own perceptions, she had gone right up to the glass and stared. But Greg had been dead for seven years; she knew that with the part of her mind that observed this stranger,

36

though she had never accepted it in that other half where the boy was still going on into the fullness of his life, still growing, so that she knew just how he had looked at fifteen, seventeen, and how he would look now at twenty.

This young man was quite unlike him. Stoop-shouldered, intense, with clothes that didn't quite fit, he was shabby, and it was the shabbiness of poverty not fashion. In his loose flannel trousers with turnups, collarless shirt and wide-brimmed felt hat, he might have been from the country or from another era. Country people dressed like that. He looked, she thought, the way young men had looked in her childhood, men who were out of work.

Thin, pale, with the sleeves half-rolled on his wiry forearms, he must have seen her come up to the glass and note his presence, but he wasn't at all intimidated.

Yes, that's what he reminded her of: the Depression years, and those men, one-armed or one-legged some of them, others dispiritingly whole, who had haunted the street corners of her childhood, wearing odd bits of uniform with their civilian castoffs and offering bootlaces or pencils for sale. Sometimes when you answered the back doorbell, one of them would be standing there on the step. A job was what he was after: mowing or cleaning out drains, or scooping the leaves from a blocked downpipe, or mending shoes – anything to save him from mere charity. When there was, after all, no job to be done, they simply stood, those men, as this man stood, waiting for the offer to be made of a cup of tea with a slice of bread and jam, or the scrapings from a bowl of dripping, or if you could spare it, the odd sixpence – it didn't matter what or how much, since the offering was less important in itself than the unstinting recognition of their presence, and beyond that, a commonness between you. As a child she had stood behind lattice doors in the country town she came from and watched transactions between her mother and those men, and had thought to herself: *This is one of the rituals. There is a way of doing this so that a man's pride can be saved, but also your own.* But when she grew up the Depression was over. Instead, there was the war. She had never had to use any of that half-learned wisdom.

She walked out now onto the patio and looked at the young man, with just air rather than plate glass between them.

He still wasn't anyone she recognized, but he had moved slightly, and as she stood there silently observing – it must have been for a good while – she saw that he continued to move. He was turning his face to the sun. He was turning with the sun, as a plant does, and she thought that if he decided to stay and put down roots she might get used to him. After all, why a buddleia or a flowering quince and not a perfectly ordinary young man?

She went back into the house and decided to go on with her housework. The house didn't need doing, since there were just the two of them, but each day she did it just the same. She began with the furniture in the lounge, dusting and polishing, taking care not to touch the electronic chess-set that was her husband's favourite toy and which she was afraid of disturbing – no, she was actually afraid of *it*. Occupying a low table of its own, and surrounded by lamps, it was a piece of equipment that she had thought of at first as an intruder and regarded now as a difficult but permanent guest. It announced the moves it wanted made in a dry dead voice, like a man speaking with a peg on his nose or through a thin coffin-lid; and once, in the days when she still resented it, she had accidentally touched it off. She had already turned away to the sideboard when the voice came, flat and dull, dropping into the room one of its obscure directives: *Queen to King's Rook five*; as if something in the room, some object she had always thought of as tangible but without life, had suddenly decided to make contact with her and were announcing a cryptic need. Well, she had got over that.

She finished the lounge, and without going to the window again went right on to the bathroom, got down on her knees, and cleaned all round the bath, the shower recess, the basin and lavatory; then walked straight through to the lounge-room and looked.

He was still there and had turned a whole quarter-circle. She saw his slight figure with the slumped shoulders in profile. But what was happening? He cast no shadow. His shadow had disappeared. The iron tap cast a shadow and the young man didn't. It took her a good minute, in which she was genuinely alarmed, to see that what she had taken for the shadow of the tap was a dark patch of lawn where the water dripped. So that was all right. It was midday.

She did a strange thing then. Without having made any decision about it, she went into the kitchen, gathered the ingredients, and made up a batch of spiced biscuits with whole peanuts in them; working fast with the flour, the butter, the spice, and forgetting herself in the pleasure of getting the measurements right by the feel of the thing, the habit.

They were biscuits that had no special name. She had learned to make them when she was just a child, from a girl they had had in the country. The routine of mixing and spooning the mixture on to greaseproof paper let her back into a former self whose motions were lighter, springier, more sure of ends and means. She hadn't made these biscuits – hadn't been able to bring herself to make them – since Greg died. They were his favourites. Now, while they were cooking and filling the house with their spicy sweetness, she did another thing she hadn't intended to do. She went to Greg's bedroom at the end of the hall, across from where she and Jack slept, and began to take down from the wall the pennants he had won for swimming, the green one with gold lettering, the purple one, the blue, and his lifesaving certificates, and laid them carefully on the bed. She brought a carton from under the stairs and packed them in the bottom. Then she cleared the bookshelf and took down the model planes, and put them in the carton as well. Then she removed from a drawer of the desk a whole mess of things: propelling pencils and pencil-stubs, rubber-bands, tubes of glue, a pair of manacles, a pack of playing cards that if you were foolish enough to take one gave you an electric shock. She put all these things into the carton, along with a second drawerful of magazines and loose-leaf notebooks, and carried the carton out. Then she took clean sheets and made the bed.

By now the biscuits were ready to be taken from the oven. She counted them, there were twenty-three. Without looking up to where the young man was standing, she opened the kitchen window and set them, sweetly smelling of spice, on the window ledge. Then she went back and sat on Greg's bed while they cooled.

She looked round the blank walls, wondering, now that she had stripped them, what a young man of twenty-eight might have filled them with, and discovered with a pang that she could not guess.

It was then that another figure slipped into her head.

In her middle years at school there had been a boy who sat two desks in front of her called Stevie Caine. She had always felt sorry for him because he lived alone with an aunt and was poor. The father had worked for the railways but lost his job after a crossing accident and killed himself. It was Stevie Caine this young man reminded her of. His shoulders too had been narrow and stooped, his face unnaturally pallid, his wrists bony and raw. Stevie's hair was mouse-coloured and had stuck out in wisps behind the ears; his auntie cut it, they said, with a pudding-basin. He smelled of scrubbing-soap. Too poor to go to the pictures on Saturday afternoons, or to have a radio and hear the serials, he could take no part in the excited chatter and argument through which they were making a world for themselves. When they ate their lunch he sat by himself on the far side of the yard, and she alone had guessed the reason: it was because the metal lunch-tin that his father had carried to the Railway had nothing in it, or at best a slice of bread and dripping. But poor as he was, Stevie had not been resentful – that was the thing that had most struck her. She felt he ought to have been. And his face sometimes, when he was excited and his Adam's apple worked up and down, was touched at the cheekbones with such a glow of youthfulness and joy that she had wanted to reach out and lay her fingers very gently to his skin and feel the warmth, but thought he might misread the tenderness that filled her (which certainly included him but was for much more beside) as girlish infatuation or, worse still, pity. So she did nothing.

Stevie Caine had left school when he was just fourteen and went like his father to work at the Railway. She had seen him sometimes in a railway worker's uniform, black serge, wearing a black felt hat that made him look bonier than ever about the cheekbones and chin and carrying the same battered lunch-tin. Something in his youthful refusal to be bitter or subdued had continued to move her. Even now, years later, she could see the back of his thin neck, and might have leaned out, no longer caring if she was misunderstood, and laid her hand to the chapped flesh.

When he was eighteen he had immediately joined up and was immediately killed; she had seen it in the papers – just the name.

It was Stevie Caine this young man resembled, as she had last seen him in the soft hat and railway worker's serge waistcoat, with the sleeves rolled on his stringy arms. There had been nothing between them, but she had never forgotten. It had to do, as she saw it, with the two forms of injustice: the one that is cruel but can be changed, and the other kind – the tipping of a thirteen-year-old boy off the saddle of his bike into a bottomless pit – that cannot; with that and an empty lunch-tin that she would like to have filled with biscuits with whole peanuts in them that have no special name.

She went out quickly now (the young man was still there on the lawn beyond the window) and counted the biscuits, which were cool enough to be put into a barrel. There were twenty-three, just as before.

He stayed there all afternoon and was still there among the deepening shadows when Jack came in. She was pretty certain now of what he was but didn't want it confirmed – and how awful if you walked up to someone, put your hand out to see if it would go through him, and it didn't.

They had tea, and Jack, after a shy worried look in her direction, which she affected not to see, took one of the biscuits and slowly ate it. She watched. He was trying not to show how broken up he was. Poor Jack!

Twenty-two.

Later, while he sat over his chess set and the mechanical voice told him what moves he should make on its behalf, she ventured to the window and peered through. It was, very gently, raining, and the streetlights were blurred and softened. Slow cars passed, their tyres swishing in the wet. They pushed soft beams before them.

The young man stood there in the same spot. His shabby clothes were drenched and stuck to him. The felt hat was also drenched, and droplets of water had formed at the brim, on one side filled with light, a half-circle of brilliant dots.

'Mustn't it be awful,' she said, 'to be out there on a night like this and have nowhere to go? There must be so many of them. Just standing about in the rain, or sleeping in it.'

Something in her tone, which was also flat, but filled with an emotion that deeply touched and disturbed him, made the man leave his game and come to her side. They stood together a moment facing the dark wall of glass, then she turned, looked him full in the face and did something odd: she reached out towards him and her hand bumped against his ribs – that is how he thought of it: a bump. It was the oddest thing! Then impulsively, as if with sudden relief, she kissed him.

I have so much is what she thought to herself.

Next morning, alone again , she cleared away the breakfast things, washed and dried up, made a grocery list. Only then did she go to the window.

It was a fine clear day and there were two of them, alike but different; both pale and hopeless looking, thin-shouldered, un-shaven, wearing shabby garments, but not at all similar in feature. They did not appear to be together. That is, they did not stand close, and there was nothing to suggest that they were in league or that the first had brought the other along or summoned him up. But there were two of them just the same, as if some *process* were involved. Tomorrow, she guessed, there would be four, and the next day sixteen; and at last – for there must be millions to be drawn on – so many that there would be no place on the lawn for them to stand, not even the smallest blade of grass. They would spill out into the street, and from there to the next street as well – there would be no room for cars to get through or park – and so it would go on till the suburb, and the city and a large part of the earth was covered. This was just the start.

She didn't feel at all threatened. There was nothing in either of these figures that suggested menace. They simply stood. But she thought she would refrain from telling Jack till he noticed it himself. Then they would do together what was required of them.

SORROWS AND
SECRETS

'You've fallen on yer feet, son, you're in luck. This is the university 'v hard knocks you've dropped into but I've taken a fancy to yer. I'll see to it the knocks aren't too solid.'

It was the foreman speaking, in a break on the boy's first day. The five of them had knocked off just at eleven and were sitting about on logs, or sprawled on the leaves of the clearing, having a smoke and drinking coppery tea.

The foreman himself had made the tea. Gerry had followed him about, watching carefully how he should trawl the billy through the scummy water so that what he drew was good and clear, how to make a fire, how the billy should hang, when to put in the tea and how much. The foreman was particular. From now on Gerry would make the tea. The foreman was confident he would make it well and that he would do all right at the rest of his work as well. The foreman was taking an interest.

He was a sandy, sad-eyed fellow of maybe forty, with a grey flannel vest instead of a shirt. Gerry felt immediately that he was a man to be trusted, though not an easy man to get along with, and guessed that it was his own newness that made him so ready on this occasion to talk. With the others he was reserved, even hostile. When they sat down to their tea he had set himself apart and then indicated, with a gesture of his tin mug, that Gerry should sit close by. Gerry observed, through the thin smoke of the fire, that the other fellows were narrowly watching, but with no more than tolerant amusement, as they licked their cigarette-papers and rolled them between thumb and finger. As if to say: 'Ol' Claude's found an ear to bash.'

They were quiet fellows in their thirties, rough-looking but clean-shaven, and one of them was a quarter-cast called Slinger. The others were Charlie and Kev. Gerry was to share a hut with them. The foreman Claude had his own sleeping quarters on the track to the thunderbox. He was permanent.

They were working for a Mister McPhearson, a shadowy figure known only to Claude; and even Claude had seen him less often than he let on. They were on McPhearson's land, using McPhearson's equipment, and it was his timber they were felling and to him, finally, that Claude was responsible. His name was frequently on the foreman's lips, especially when there was some question of authority beyond which there could be no appeal. 'Don' ast me, ast McPhearson,' he'd say. And then humorously: 'If you can find 'im.' Or: 'Well now, there you'd be dealin' with McPhearson. That'd be his department,' and there was something in Claude's smile as he said it that was sly. Inside, he was laughing outright.

Claude had a preference for mysteries. If McPhearson's name hadn't been stamped so clearly on all their equipment they might have decided he was one of Claude's humorous inventions.

Gerry had been sent here to learn, the hard way, about life. It was his father's intention that he should discover at first hand that his advantages (meaning Vine Brothers, which was one of the biggest machine-tool operations in the state) were accidental, had not been earned by him and were in no way deserved; they did not constitute a proof of superiority. His mother spoiled him, as she did all of them. She had let him believe he was special. That's what his father said. He was out here to learn that he was not. The job had been arranged through a fellow his father knew at the Golf Club, who happened also to know McPhearson. Claude had started off by asking questions, as if he suspected a connection between Gerry and the Boss that had not yet been revealed, but there was none. Just that friend of his father's at the Club.

They worked hard and Gerry kept up with them. He didn't want it to show that what for them was hard necessity was for him a rich boy's choice. All day their saws buzzed, their sweat flew in the forest, and at night they were tired.

There wasn't much talk. Gerry, who usually fell asleep immediately they'd eaten, and had to be shaken to go to bed, got very little of the wisdom of the wider world out of what was said when they had swallowed their stew, drunk their tea, and were just sitting out in the smell of timber and burnt leaves under the stars.

'You should watch out f' loose women,' one of the fellows said once. He seemed to be joking.

'I been watchin' out for 'em,' Slinger said. 'There ain't none around 'ere that I been able to discover.' He looked off into the shifting, stirring dark.

'No,' the third fellow said bitterly, 'it ain't the loose women you need t' watch out for, it's the moral ones. A moral woman'll kill a man's spirit. The others – ' But he bit off the rest of what he might have to tell. It went on silently behind his eyes, and the others, out of respect for something personal, fell into their own less heavy forms of silence.

It was Claude who provided most of the talk.

'One time,' Claude told, 'I was stoppin' at this boarding-house in Brisbane. I was workin' at the abatoors then, it was just after the war. Well, at the boarding-house there was this refugee-bloke, an' sometimes after tea, if I din' feel like playin' poker or listenin' t' Willy Fernell and Mo, this bloke an' me'd sit out on the front step in the cool. Not talkin' much – I wasn' much of a talker in them days. But I s'pose he reckoned I was sort of sympathetic, I din' rib 'im like the rest. He was a Dutchman, or a Finn – one of that lot. Maybe a Balt. Anyway a thin feller with very good manners, and exceptionally clean – exceptionally. On'y 'e was as mad as a meat axe. I mean, one day 'e'd be that quiet you couldn' get a word out of 'im, and the next 'e'd be on the booze and ravin'. 'E kept the booze under his bed. Vodka. Talked like a drain when 'e was pissed, an' all stuff you couldn' make sense of. He was hidin' from someone – some other lot, I never did find out who – you know what these New Australians are like. Look 'ere mate, I'd tell 'im, there's no politics here, this is Australia. But 'e'd just look at me as if I was

45

soft or somethink. And in fact he was loaded – God knows what 'e didn' have stacked away, jewellery an' that – I saw some of it – 'e could of lived in any place he liked – at Lennon's even. 'E'd be in his sixties now, that bloke – I often wonder what happened to 'im . . . Anyway, we were sittin' out on the step one night, jus' cool in our shirtsleeves, havin' a bit of a smoke, when the cicadas start up. "What's that?" 'e says, jumpin' to 'is feet. "Cicadas," I tell 'im. "Chicago?" he says, all wild-eyed, "the *gangsters?*" I had t' laugh, but it was pathetic jus' the same. The poor bugger thought 'e'd got 'imself to America, thought it was machine-guns. Never seemed t' know where 'e was half the time. You'd think a boarding-house at Dutton Park 'd impress itself on *anyone,* but not him. "Chicago," 'e says, "the gangsters!" God knows what sort of things 'e'd been through – *over there* – I mean, you can't tell, can you? You look at a bloke jus' sittin' there an' you can't tell. There's a lot of misery about. You've only got t' go into some o' them boarding-houses and see what blokes 'ave got in ports under their beds. Old newspapers, bottles, stones. It'd surprise you. It'd surprise anyone.'

Gerry listened to Claude's tales. They were interesting but he could make nothing of them; they appeared to tell more than they told. There was a quality in Claude's voice that asked for something more than interest, and it was just this that Gerry resisted. He wanted Claude to be the foreman, only that, and preferred the dour but dignified silence of the other men, who if they had stories to tell kept them entirely to themselves.

The hut where Claude lived was divided by a partition into sleeping-quarters and storeroom. On one wall of the storeroom there were tools, very neatly arranged on hooks. They might have borne labels and been mistaken at first sight for a wall display in a folk museum, or for the elaborate fan shapes and sunbursts that native weapons assume when they have been stripped of their power of violence and become flowerlike – till you examine the points.

'I like t' see things in their place,' Claude explained. 'Order at a glance.' And he glanced up from where he was sitting at a desk doing McPhearson's accounts.

He wore half-glasses and was peering over the straight tops of them. It made his eyes a weaker blue and gave him, for all his toughness, a scholarly look, like a failed monk. To his left were heavy ledgers, and immediately before him a pile of accounts waiting to be pushed down hard on a spike. Beyond, at the far end of the room, which was dark, Gerry could see the shelves of foodstuff – jars, tins, packets – from which Claude provided the ingredients for their meals, including a whole shelf of Claude's own homemade chutney.

Claude had surprised Gerry the first time he went there by what seemed like an act of disloyalty.

'Here,' he had offered impetuously, 'have a jar of peanut paste. On the house! McPhearson won't miss it. He's swimmin' in peanut paste that man. An' smoked salmon, they tell me.' And when Gerry politely refused: 'What about a packet a' Bandaids?'

Claude shrugged his shoulders and looked disappointed, and Gerry was left with a puzzle. The foreman was strict but inconsistent.

As for the other side of the partition, where Claude slept, Gerry saw that only once, when Claude cut his leg, bled badly, and sent him off to get a fresh pair of shorts. There were cuttings from newspapers pinned to the bare boards – racehorses – and on the desk a box of old stereopticon plates that Claude had already told him about and promised to show: pictures from round the world. 'You can stand right at the edge and see the waters of Niagara come thunderin' down – I tell yer, it's marvellous. I've stood there f' hours and even heard the noise of it. Imagined that, of course. The pyramids, the Taj Mahal, George the Fifth's Jubilee – you name it! A man can go round the world in 'is head with one a' these stereopticons, and it don't cost a brass razoo.'

Gerry had looked round the narrow room, tried to make something of it – tried to make Claude of it – but saw nothing more than he already knew. He thought of his own room at home. He was untidy and his mother complained, but did his disorder reveal any more of what was going on in his head than Claude's fastidious habit of setting everything in its place? He had been able to tell

Gerry, even through the pain of his wound, just where those clean shorts would be: in the second drawer to the left. Gerry had gone straight to them.

One day Claude came down to where he was working and asked him to go to town on a message. The town was twelve miles away. He was to go on Claude's two-stroke and deliver a letter. Claude drew a rough map of the town, showed him where the house was, and gave him very precise instructions about how he should open the gate, go up the four steps and ring the doorbell – three long rings and then, after a pause, two short ones. 'Like this,' Claude explained, tapping it out on a metal cup. He was to leave the motorbike in the main street and go the rest of the way – it wasn't more than a hundred yards – on foot. Claude emphasized that he was putting great trust in the boy, and embarrassed perhaps by the air of mystery he had created, suggested that Gerry needn't hurry back; he could take time off if he wanted to have a milkshake at the Greek's. The message was in a plain white envelope with neither name nor address.

The ride into town was a pleasant one. After three weeks of work Gerry was happy to have this time away, to feel released into his own body again and to be made free of the landscape and of the hot summer day.

The early part of the trip was rough. A narrow trail led upward between thick-set pines. But he emerged at last on to a high rolling plateau where the clouds rode close overhead, struck a gravel road, then two miles before the town a stretch of bitumen. He opened his shirt and took the full thrust of the air. Crossing bridges over dry streams he heard the sound they made as he rattled across them, the *slog slog slog* of concrete balusters, a regular beating in his ear, and remembered the different rhythm – three longs, a pause and two shorts – that Claude had tapped out on the cup. Its meaning didn't concern him. It was Claude's business, or maybe it was McPhearson's. He was a messenger. He felt extraordinarily light-hearted. Perhaps because this was the first occasion in so long that he had been on his own, but also because, small as it might be, he was being entrusted with something. He had recently discovered, in the furthest reaches of himself, a capacity for what he thought of as noble action and was concerned now that it should find its proper form in the world; that when the occasion arose (as it surely must) that would demand the full stretch of his powers, he would recognize and meet it.

The problem of course was in the recognition. He was inexperienced but not romantic, and had perceived clearly enough that heroic occasions do not come ready-made, that they spring into existence only when they are grasped. You would need imagination as well as pluck. Two years ago he might have seen himself through drifts of gun-smoke bearing the colours, or as a dispatch-rider in one of the wars, vaulting shell holes on a BSA. But the next occasion wouldn't be like it, and any moment, even the most commonplace, might be either the call or the first step towards it. You had to be on the alert, and believe that when the opportunity came you would be ready for it.

All this was part of his most secret life. He let it out now that he was alone and flaring along a bitumen road – in the open air, under leaves, in sunlight; and all the more because for the last weeks he had held back, and tried among the others to seem acceptable, ordinary.

He came into the town over a bridge. Kids were swimming in the last of the season's water, among thick willows. He stopped the bike halfway across, and still easily astride it, leaned over the railings to watch. Slim bodies swung out on a knotted rope and went flying head-over-heels, their cries cut off in a splash. The sight pleased him. He was just out of that stage himself and might have allowed himself to regret it, but had set himself in the direction of manhood. He rode on into town, parked the bike, and was thirsty enough after his ride to consider going straight to the Greek's. But no, he told himself, Duty first. I'll deliver the message and have the milkshake afterwards.

The town was small and sleepy, but after his weeks up at the camp seemed to him to be bustling with life. Women clicked along the pavement in their high heels. A girl riding by on a bike with her skirt up looked back over her shoulder, and he was taken again by the variousness of the world and the number of paths that were open in each moment of it. Later, that was for later. With the envelope safe in his shirt pocket he turned out of the main street with its row of two-storeyed buildings that went on for another quarter of a mile, all pubs, banks, general stores, bakeries, into the dusty streets behind. Crossed one, then another, till he found the name he wanted, and was about to consult numbers when he was hailed from a low verandah.

'Hey! Givvus a lift, wilya sonny?'

The man was holding one end of a genoa-velvet lounge as if he had been standing there maybe all morning, waiting for someone to come along, as Gerry had, and take the other.

Gerry hesitated – this was an interruption – but didn't see how he could refuse. The man looked expectant. The lounge, with one end on the ground and the other in the air, was ridiculous. After a moment's hesitation he took it up as directed, walked backwards a few paces and helped the man push it on to the back of a lorry.

'The rest is a walkover,' the man told him. He was a tall fellow with teeth missing, wearing nothing but football shorts. 'I'll bring the armchair, you get the smokers' stands an' the side table.'

He followed the man into the house and they cleared the front room and loaded it, then carried out of a second room a dining table, a sideboard, six chairs and a framed oil painting of the Alps. The lorry by now had about as much as it would carry. Gerry held the other end of several ropes while the man strained, cursed, knotted. Then, with a casual, 'Thanks, son, I'll do the same f' you some time,' he climbed into the cabin and drove slowly away. He had left the door of the house standing wide open.

Gerry wondered as he walked away if he mightn't have been assisting at a burglary. But what else could he have done? He noted the number of the house he had helped strip, in case there were questions later, and saw now that the one he wanted was just three doors off on the other side. He crossed, opened the gate with as little sound as possible, went on up the steps, pushed the bell three times as Claude had directed, waited, then rang twice more. Almost immediately a curtain twitched aside in one of the front windows and a girl's face appeared. Then she was at the open door.

'For Christ sake!' she spat out. 'What are you playin' at?' She gave an alarmed glance behind him and to both sides. 'Who th' fuck are you?'

Barefoot, hastily wrapped in a gown with explosive red-and-gold flowers all over it, she smelled of soap and had the misty look of a woman who had come fresh from the bath.

The messenger for a moment failed to find his tongue, and she softened a little at his youth, at the way he flushed, and the movement of his eyes towards the mysterious darkness behind her.

She turned her head as if following his gaze, and said over her shoulder: 'It's nothing. Just some kid.' She gave him a look, half-knowing, half-ironical, but no longer alarmed. 'Watcha want, son?'

'I've brought this,' Gerry told her coldly, showing the envelope. 'It's from Claude.'

She took the envelope, tore it open, glanced quickly at both sides of the single sheet and then burst out laughing. She began to close the door.

'Isn't there an answer?' Gerry asked foolishly.

'Are you kidding? How would you answer that?'

She showed him both sides of the page and they stood at the half-open door with the blank sheet between them.

'Piss off,' she said, not urgently: and the door was closed in his face.

He rode back fast, his face still burning. He hadn't after all stopped at the Greek's, and when he came bumping into the camp and parked the bike, and saw Claude coming down to meet him, would have turned away if he could and found work to do.

Claude came at him sideways. He screwed one eye up as if squinting at sunlight.

'Well,' he said shyly, 'how was the trip? Bike behave? Dja find the house alright?'

He answered Claude's questions, he rendered account; but would not, for all Claude's soft-talk, be sweetened.

Yes, he had rung the bell. Yes, it was a woman who had answered. She had been wearing a kimono. No, he hadn't seen into the house. Yes, he had delivered the envelope. What had she done? She'd laughed, that's what, and there was no answer.

Claude patted him on the shoulder, but when their eyes met he looked away, and Gerry, who had been glaring till that moment, was glad of it. There was something between them suddenly of which they were both, but for different reasons, ashamed.

'Thanks, Gerry,' Claude said wearily. 'Thanks, mate. You done well. If I ever had another message I'd –'

He broke off, as if he had heard Gerry's fierce, unspoken Not me, you wouldn't! Not again!

'Come 'n have tea,' Claude was saying in his smallest voice, 'I made puftaloons. They're yer favourite.' He looked uncomfortably large in his grey flannel vest, but also beaten, and his tone was so wheedling and auntlike, so keen to make amends, that Gerry was torn between contempt and a kind of shameful pity. Without ceasing to be aggrieved he relented, and allowed himself to be drawn away.

'That's the style,' the man said, as if it were Gerry who had to be got over a rough patch. 'I make good puftaloons, even if I say so meself. Learned from a Chinese. Little feller with only one arm. It was out Charleville way . . . ' And he was off on another of his tales.

That night they got drunk. Claude sat out in the moonlight on a stump, sucking a bottle of whisky, and the others, out of delicacy, kept away. Slinger the quarter-caste played his mouth organ.

'Wife-trouble,' Kev whispered, and nodded his head seriously.

Gerry didn't admit that he knew something of that already; had been out earlier in the day, subjecting the woman to some mild terrorism.

Kev, staring off into the darkness, was lost in his own story.

Is life so sad then? Gerry asked himself. And was aware, with a sharpness he had not felt before, of the immensity of the darkness that surrounded them: all those leaves holding up individual fragments of it shaped exactly like themselves, the grassblades taking it down into their roots, the birds folding it away under their wings. Sorrows and secrets. All these men had stories, were dense with the details of their lives, but kept them in the dark. Only odd words broke surface and spoke for more than could be said.

'That's a nice tune, Slinger. I remember that one from the navy,' Kev said. 'Wartime.'

'Wrong colour f' the navy,' Slinger let out between chords, barely breaking the line of what he was playing.

Claude meanwhile had gone off, and when he appeared again it was from the door of his storeroom. He was carrying jars of the homemade chutney they had eaten at every meal Gerry had had here. 'Mango chutney,' Claude had explained, 'off me own trees. I got two big 'uns in the back yard, with more mangoes than you could eat in a month a' Sundays. I make a big batch every year.'

Now, armful after armful, he was carrying the labelled jars out of the storeroom and setting them down on the moonlit earth. The others fell silent and watched. He stacked them solemnly, neatly, so that they made a high but solid pyramid, and when the last one was out he closed and locked the storeroom door.

'Now we'll have some fun,' he told them.

Standing bent-kneed and with his feet firmly apart, he balanced a jar on the palm of his hand, took it back over his shoulder, and hurled it against the storehouse wall. Moonlight splintered, and the dark golden stuff with its chunks of stringy fruit rolled slowly down.

'Here Slinger, Kev, Gerry – have a go!' He stooped and hurled another. 'It's all right boys, this is on me, it's my bloody chutney. Nothin' t' do with McPhearson. I don't account t' him f' chutney.'

But the others, suddenly sober, did not join in. At last one of them went up to him.

'Come on, mate, time t' turn in,' he said. 'We've got a heavy day.'

It ended then. They went to bed. But were woken some time later by what sounded like another jar of chutney being smashed against the storeroom wall. They all started up at once and trooped out in their underpants to see what it was. The clearing was empty, still. It was Kev who knocked, with embarrassed politeness, at the door to Claude's hut and pushed it open. They heard him gasp.

'Aw, the poor bugger!'

It hadn't sounded like a shot.

There was a note, and beside it an envelope, exactly like the one Gerry had carried earlier in the day. It was addressed to the woman and the house in town. The note asked Gerry to deliver it, and on this occasion to drive right up to the house on the bike. But when the police came they took charge of the envelope along with the body.

The remaining jars of chutney, all shot through with gold as the sun struck them, were still stacked in a ruined pyramid in the grass. The police found them difficult to fit into the picture, and the others, faced with them and with the dried stains on the storehouse wall, which looked almost natural, as if the wood had experienced a new flow of thick golden sap, turned away in common embarrassment. At last one of the policemen unlocked the storehouse door with Claude's keys, and Gerry and Charlie took the jars back and set them neatly, darkly, on the shelf.

The sight of the storeroom, with everything fastidiously in place and even the chutney now restored, unnerved Gerry. If he were to go now into that space behind the partition, and note every detail, and add to it the final disordering of all its objects by the shot, nothing would be revealed, he thought, or added to what he knew.

He watched the younger of the two policemen slip Claude's letter into his breast-pocket. The policeman wore a uniform: boots, cap, shirt with epaulettes and a flash – he was official. He would ring the bell just once. And if the door wasn't answered immediately he would ring a second time, and again and again until it was.

THAT ANTIC JEZEBEL

Climbing to her seat in the organ gallery, up three flights of stairs, was such an arduous business, and she was so slow nowadays, that Clay had to begin early, even before the warning bells were sounded. She hated the thought of arriving breathless, of being locked out, or of looking, on the way up, like an old girl in need of aid. 'He's cooked his goose – let him lie in it'; that was one of her sayings. Messy of course, but life is, you got used to it.

Clay McHugh had learned her survival tactics in Europe between the wars. She had studied there how to present an appearance that was never less than elegant and might be mistaken by snobs, and by the undiscerning and unworldly, for affluence. You lived in the best part of town, had one outfit of perfect cut that went to the cleaners each week, one piece of jewellery, and you never let anyone past the door.

Her present apartment was at Elizabeth Bay and she had spent all she had on it. Within its walls, among the last of her loot, she practised a frugality that would have surprised her neighbours and made social workers, and other Nosey Parkers, cry famine. Clay despised such terms. She ate a great deal of boiled rice, was careful with the lights, and on the pretext of keeping trim, she walked rather than took the bus. Her one outfit was black; her one piece of jewellery a chain of intimidating weight that chimed rather than tinkled but was too plain to suggest ostentation. Hung with mint-gold coins, seals and medallions, it provoked questions and the answers told a story – in fact several stories, but never all. There was, each time, a little something-left-over.

This chain was her *curriculum vitae*. She shook it when she needed to remind herself that whatever hole she was now in, she had once been in a different one and this was her choice. The chain spoke of attachments: of men young and old, back there in Europe, who had wanted at one time or another to present her with their blue eyes, their lives, their titles, or with little flats in Paris or London or country houses near Antwerp or Rome – all of which, for good reason, she had declined. The men had slipped away, leaving only a family seal or rare coin or medal. The weight on her wrist was bearable and she thought of it as a tribute to her intention to keep free.

That was one way of putting it. Put another way, you might say that the men had escaped and that these coins were the price they'd been willing to pay. Clay looked at it different ways on different occasions, but mostly she thought of herself as having come out of all this – of *life* – as well as could be expected: that is, badly. But her freedom was important to her. All those dull dogs and bushy-tailed buffers, if they were still kicking, would be as old now as herself. She would, if she had accepted their offers, be no more than an expensive nursemaid to an old man's incontinence – though she was not without affection and she wouldn't have complained, even of that, after a lifetime of some other devotion, if it had been her fate; or if the right man – Karel for instance – had asked it of her. Things had turned out otherwise, that's all. She was lying with the goose.

Besides, she told herself in her scarier moments, I'll soon be in that state myself, except that I won't be. I won't hang around to get up at three in the morning like poor Grandma and make scones for people who've been dead for thirty years. I'll finish it first. I'll take the bun and the pills . . .

(This grandmother had lived with them. As a grown girl of fifteen she had been sent out, burning with shame before the neighbours, but also before the old woman herself, to bring her in when she went aimlessly wandering. On several occasions that now seemed like one, they had stood shouting beside a fence in the overpowering smell of honeysuckle. The old woman whined, screeched, wheedled, tried to shake off the grip on her wrist; dogs barked, children stared, other old women shook their heads behind blinds – she could still feel the pain, the humiliation of it. But the centre of the occasion had shifted now from the unwilling and angry girl to the wilful old woman, who with her hair awry and her gown open stood barefoot under the streetlamp saying over and over 'Why are you doing this to me?' The old woman was herself.)

She shook her wrist and the chain clanked against the gallery rail, as leaning forward she allowed her eye, which was sharp, to sweep the crowded amphitheatre.

Eleanor had just come in, high up in the stalls. Tall, in an emerald cloak, she was waiting for the people in her row to get up and let her through.

How like her! There was stacks of room up there, not like these gallery boxes – stacks of it! But Eleanor continued to stand, and when at last the whole row had risen to its feet, the silly woman, holding her cloak about her, moved through, gracefully inclining her head and smiling and thanking people. Settled at last, with the cloak thrown back for later, when the air-conditioning would turn the place into an ice-box, she looked about; then cast her gaze upward to the gallery and waved.

Clay immediately relented. Oh God, she told herself, I'm such a *bitch*. It was touching really, Eleanor's little wave – a real leap in the dark. Too vain to wear glasses, and half-blind by habit (as who wouldn't be after forty years with the dreaded doctor) she could barely see her face in the glass.

Clay produced in response one of her brisk salutes, a real one made by bringing two fingers of her right hand up to the temple and flicking them sharply away. It was her trade-mark; from the days when she had modelled little suits of a military cut for Molyneux in Paris and was considered a sport. It too was a leap in the dark since Eleanor couldn't see it. But she made the gesture just the same – as an acknowledgment to herself of the old, the unkillable Clay McHugh, since there was, God knows, so little left of her.

(She had taken to avoiding herself in mirrors and in ghostly shop-windows; her eyes were too sharp, she hadn't, like Eleanor, developed the habit of not-seeing-clearly-any-more. But at some point back there she had let her attention wander, lost her grip on things, and the spirit of disintegration had got in. Well, she was fighting it – tooth and claw – she was holding on; she got tired, that's all. Your attention wandered. You got tired.)

She came quickly to the alert now. Eleanor was making a play in the air with her fingers that meant they should meet later and share a taxi home. They would – they always did – and Eleanor, who was generous and tactfully tactless, would see to it that they did not share the fare.

They were neighbours. Eleanor, Mrs Adrian Murphy, lived in a unit-block three doors from her own, and once a week, on Fridays, they went down in the Daimler (Eleanor drove only in daylight now) and had coffee together: down among the heavy-eyed Viennese, all reading air-mail papers that were two weeks old, and those deeper exiles who had been born right here, in Burwood or Gulgong or Innisfail, North Queensland, but were dying of hunger for a few crumbs of Sacher Torte and of estrangement from a life they had never known. What a place! What a country!

Years ago, in Brisbane, where they had been at the same convent school, she and Eleanor Ure had hated one another. 'That stuck up goody two-shoes' was the phrase she found herself repeating in her twelve-year-old's voice; though she couldn't recall how Eleanor, who had been mousey, could have deserved it – not then. It fitted her better twenty years later when the dreaded doctor appeared.

But that period too had passed; and now, with nearly sixty years between them and the girls they once were, she could accept Eleanor Murphy for what she was: a spoiled and frightened woman, too insistent on her own dignity, but generous, loyal, and very nearly these days a friend.

That first winter after they found themselves neighbours, Eleanor had slipped and broken her leg. Clay had gone across each afternoon to sit with her: not in the spirit of a little nursing-sister – she had none of that – but in a spirit of brisk cheerfulness, of keeping one's stoic end up, that revived the bossy schoolgirl in her. Eleanor was happy to be organized. They spent the afternoons playing cards (rummy) while the westering light touched with Queensland colours the baskets of maidenhair and the tree-orchids and staghorns of Eleanor's rainforest loggia, and Mrs Thring, who came in to clean, and who served when Eleanor entertained, made them scones and tea.

Things had levelled between them. She was no longer 'that Clay McHugh', unmarried and trailing clouds of dangerous appeal. And Eleanor, with the dreaded doctor gone, was no more the gilded and girlish dependent of a Household Word. They were alone, alive (widowed or not, what did it matter?) and had no one close but one another.

(Eleanor in fact had a son whom she doted on, worried over and never mentioned; a forty-four-year-old hippy and no-hoper called Aidan, for God's sake! who wore beads, wrote unpublishable poetry, had two broken marriages behind him, and lived in a rainforest – a real one – on sunflower-seeds, bananas and old rope. Eleanor's bedroom was full of photographs of him when he was an angelic six-year-old. Clay knew all this, but was meant not to. There were days when all Eleanor had to say in the long silences between them was 'Aidan, Aidan, Aidan, Aidan.' It was hard then not to cry out, 'For God's sake, Eleanor, I thought we were friends, why can't we talk about him?' 'About who?' Eleanor would have said. 'Who can you possibly mean?')

The Year of Eleanor's Leg had been followed by The Year of the Rapist. For five months their Point was at siege. The rapist specialized in high unit-blocks and only assaulted older women (they had shared, she and Eleanor, a phone code that made Eleanor at least feel safe) and had turned out to be a twenty-two-year-old cat-burglar, so round-chinned and mild-looking that nobody believed it was really him.

Clay did. Standing at the glass door to her balcony, with her old dragon-robe about her, she had come face to face with him. He was spreadeagled against the wall, his cheek flat to the bricks. There was only feet between them; he in the cold air, high up above the fig tree and its voracious flying-foxes, she safe behind glass. Below, the whole Bay was lit. The police were on to him. Their searchlights crossed and re-crossed the fern-hung balconies.

Let me in, his eyes had pleaded. He was blond, with a two-day growth that made a shadow above his lips. She shook her head.

He had smiled then and nodded; as if she were some silly old girl who could be fooled by a soft look and didn't know he was a tiger, a beast of prey, and these tower blocks were his jungle. Nervously his tongue appeared, just the tip, and slicked his lips. He was perplexed, he was thinking with it.

If she hesitated a moment then it wasn't because she was fooled but because she saw his animal mind at work. They were a pair. She too had been 'out there'.

She didn't let him in. Another night she might have, it wasn't final; but not that one. She stood and watched the searchlight play across the balcony; go on, back-track, then stop, isolating him like an acrobat, an angel, in its glare. He had his eyes closed. He was pressing his body hard against the wall, pretending, like a child, to be invisible.

Being more vulnerable than ever at that moment she had turned quickly away . . .

So there was Eleanor, safely settled in the stalls. And there, in their box, were the Scarmans, Robert and Jeanette, who always appeared for the first half but seldom for the second. Cool ash-blonds, very still and fastidious, they tried again and again but real players never came up to what they were used to on Robert's equipment. Robert had been Karel's favourite student (that was how she knew them), but he was fonder now of Jeanette.

She caught their eye, and Jeanette made little window-cleaning motions that meant See-you-later-in-the-usual-place. (That was the Crush Bar on the harbour side.)

All this was ritual. She watched Jeanette wave to the Abrams, and the Abrams a moment later caught her own eye, and Clay gave them her salute. Then Doctor Havek, whom she had known in Paris before the war, then in Cairo, and who was now her doctor at Edgecliff, shuffled to his seat in the third row – down in Middle Europe among the garlic and ashes; but before he was seated, he too waved to the Abrams and then leaned over and shook hands with the Scorczenys, whom she had also known in Paris but had nothing to do with here.

She began to tap her foot. Karel hadn't arrived. They had spoken on Thursday – no, Friday, and he had said yes, he definitely was well enough, he would be here.

It was just before eight. Downstairs the last bleeps would be sounding, like a nasty moment in a beleaguered submarine. But the seat between the blond woman and the couple who hummed, Karel insisted, through all of Mozart and Beethoven and most of Schubert (though they were pretty well stumped by Bartók) was empty, the only one in its row.

'Would you like to see the programme?' the young man on her right was enquiring. He was a sweet rather effeminate boy who had struck up a conversation at the start of the season and chattered on now whether she answered or not. She thanked him, turned the pages politely and handed it back.

'Martinù,' the boy said with excitement. He had apple cheeks and a great deal of fluffy bronze hair.

Martinù too she had known for a time. She did not say so. She was too puzzled.

Down in the hall a character in a double-breasted suit had paused at the end of Karel's row, and after turning his head this way and that to examine the ticket, was pushing in towards the empty seat. It was a mistake – he had the wrong row; she leaned forward across the tense air to inform him.

Short, fair, balding, he pushed his way along the row, pausing frequently to excuse himself, and seemed unaware of his error. When he reached the seat at last he stood flicking it with a handkerchief, then settled. But uncomfortably, sitting too far forward, and went to work now, with the same handkerchief, on his brow. He mopped, consulted his watch, mopped again – all the time in the wrong seat; then sat with the handkerchief crumpled up in his right hand like an unhappy child, and sitting too far forward, as if his legs would not reach the ground.

It was this vision of him as an unlikely middle-aged child that gave her the clue. She saw a plump nine-year-old with sloping shoulders in front of a row of newly-planted poplars. The poplars were meant to civilize a wilderness, and the child, who wore khaki shorts and sand-shoes, was bearing a spade. It was a snapshot. He squinted into the sun. Well, those poplars now must be sixty, seventy-feet high, sending their roots to block someone's drains. And the child would be – Nicholas. Nicholas!

Her heart thumped and she half-rose to her feet. But the hall was ringing with applause now and the chamber group was trooping on, the lights were fading. Too late! There was a scraping and plucking as they tuned up, and she joined them with a hiss of desperation at her own slowness. It was loud enough for the boy who was her neighbour to swing his head in alarm. She made violent motions – no, it's nothing, nothing – and subsided into noiseless gloom.

That Nicholas. He had sided against his father, turned clean against him all those years ago, and now here he was occupying his father's seat. 'Traitor,' she wanted to shout down at him, 'you broke his heart!'

But on an abrupt and sickening change of key, old injustice and indignation gave way to alarm. Why wasn't Karel here, that was the real point. What had he said – on Friday was it? – no, Saturday. What had they talked about? What did they *ever* talk about, these days, these days! The music kept switching pace. She couldn't fit his voice to it. The violins were doing impossible things, leaping about off key, scraping below the bridge; no voice could be fitted to that! Oh my God, she thought, my God. The music was approaching a violent end. It ended. And the boy beside her held his hands clasped a moment, with his head thrown back and all his hair electrically tingling, before he joined the applause. 'Wasn't that terrific?' he breathed. Then, when she clenched her jaw at him: 'Are you all right?'

No, she was *not* all right! Where was Karel? Why hadn't he rung if he wasn't coming?

She got to her feet again, determined this time to rush down and call; but her head was filled with the sound of a phone ringing in an empty room, and she sat down again, plump, just like that, and covered her eyes. There was a hush. She steeled herself. Terrible Tchaikovsky bloomed all over the hall.

She managed to push her way through the harbourside bar without encountering Robert and Jeanette, or Eleanor, or the Abrams, and after an eternity of searching (where *was* the man? He couldn't spend the entire interval in the loo) she found him pacing up and down under the sloping panes that gave on the dark; nervously consulting his watch and looking so like the child of thirty years ago that she immediately felt thirty years younger herself.

'Nicholas!' she accused.

He looked startled. His hands jumped and opened. There was no need to introduce herself.

'Where is he?' she demanded.

The man frowned and lowered his gaze.

The worst, she thought, it's always the worst. Damn him!

He was looking desperately about for a place they could slip away to that wouldn't be loud with people, all standing too close and with glasses in their hands, shouting.

For God's sake, she thought, why doesn't he get it over with? I know already, it's only words. The stoop of his shoulders and his look of pained, concentrated concern was too irritating; she would have preferred him to be cruel. (It struck her then that all the bad news she had ever heard had come to her in public places: in railway-stations, hotel foyers, bars, or over public address systems in crowded squares. It was a mark of the century.) Go on, damn you, she thought now, say it, shout it why don't you?

At last, in desperation, he did. He tipped his balding head towards her, and with one hand cupped to his mouth, bellowed softly: 'My father died this morning. I tried to ring you. He collapsed while he was out shopping. I'm very sorry.'

The vision of spilled parcels hit her harder than she expected; and Nicholas, made bold by the fear that she too might be about to fall down in a public place, took her, not quite firmly, by the elbow, and kept up a dismal muttering.

They had become a centre of concern. The crowd about them

had drawn back. People were staring, she must have cried out. Nicholas, deeply embarrassed, was making little gestures towards them. He was explaining why he was clutching her, that it was not this that had provoked her cry. Meanwhile, to her, he was offering more complex explanations. 'You see,' he stammered, 'I found the ticket – and I – well I just didn't want the seat to be empty.'

His soft eyes appealed to her for understanding of his pious but perhaps foolish sentiment.

She did understand, and suddenly felt sorry for him – for his awkward emotion and the need to explain it, but also for his grief. But it hurt, that. They must have been closer than she had guessed, Karel and this grown-up Nicholas; who would be, of course – why had she never let herself think it? – the father of the grandchildren: of Elsa and Ross. She had known about the grandchildren – she even knew their birthdays, but had thought of them as having come to him without intermediaries. And now here he was, one of the *intermediaries*, thin, distressed, too formal, with the sweat breaking out on his bald crown – the bearer of a weight of filial piety that she did understand and which did after all do him credit, but which she felt like a knife in her bowels.

'Listen,' she said harshly, 'do you think you could find me a drink? Something good and strong. I'll be fine till you get back.'

She swayed a little but recovered. How odd it was after all the turmoil they had created – the promises, threats, curses, the real and imaginary violence – to have reached in a public place in Sydney this moment of utter aloneness: Elizabeth gone, that devout vindictive woman, now Karel also gone, and nothing left but this numbness before the brute fact. Karel! Tipped out on the pavements of a town he had never meant to live in, let alone die in, and the hot sky pulsing overhead as the angel zoomed, found his easy mark – there under the ribs – and pushed. She too felt it, the knife; and the closeness of his breath.

She looked up sharply at a gentler touch. Nicholas, with a double cognac and nothing for himself.

She smiled, thanked him, and playing the tough old girl, threw her head back and tossed it off. Then stood with the balloon resting lightly on her palm.

She looked at it – it was so fine. Tough but delicate. If she closed her fist and pressed hard enough it would splinter.

He must have felt the thought pass through her; she was surprised. He took the glass in his own pudgy fist, but had nowhere to put it.

'I'll see you home,' he was saying in that heavy, middle-European way, all breathless gallantry, that she had found absurd even in his father and which thirty years in Australia, the rough example of contemporaries, and the half mocking acquiescence of women like herself, had done nothing to change.

'No,' she said. 'The seat. You must stay.'

He looked down again and was embarrassed. 'The seat doesn't matter.'

'Oh but it does!' she said firmly. 'You've been kind enough already – Nicholas. I'll get a taxi.'

He did not insist. 'Then I'll find you one.'

Still holding the glass in one hand, and with the fingers of the other just pinching her elbow, he led her down the shallow steps. When they came to the foyer he made a wide arc towards one of the bars, and reaching in between packed shoulders, fumbled and set the thing down, grinning a little for the awkwardness of it.

At last they were in the open air. Out here she had no need of support. The night was fresh, and the sky, beyond harbour-rails and fig-trees, an electric blue. He stood with his hands clasped behind him, rocking gently on his heels.

'It seems a shame,' he began, 'that we've never – that we had to wait so long. I'm sorry.'

She shook her head. No good going into all that. Too late, too late.

But he was determined she saw, in his discreet, passionate, pedantic way, to deal with it, an image of her that must have been, like her own picture of him as a slope-shouldered child in shorts, a stereotype: the flashy homebreaker and Jezebel who had stolen his father and left him to be the little man of the house, the resentful mother's boy. Or perhaps what he was dealing with was his father's nakedness. Well, either way, either way, he was too late.

'If you don't mind,' he was saying, 'I'll call up tomorrow and see how you are. It's no trouble.'

She shook her head and made deprecating motions with her lips. What was it – kindness? – was he *kind*? More of his filial piety?

Fortunately the taxi had arrived. The driver gave her a look – some old girl who'd had too much to drink, and while Nicholas was giving him the address, she heard, as often before, the sound of a note being passed.

'Thank you,' she murmured, eager for nothing now except to be moving on in the dark.

'You all right, ol' lady?' the driver asked over his shoulder. There was mockery in his voice.

'Get stuffed,' she told the fellow. That fixed him.

Eleanor's late-night telephone voice was full of concern. 'No, no, I'm OK, no trouble – I was tired, that's all. How was the Schoenberg?' Then, because she was tired of making mysteries, and because sooner or later it would have to be said, she let a voice that was not quite her own announce flatly: 'Karel died this morning – a heart attack. In the street . . .' Poor Eleanor! 'No, no, I'm OK – I promise. Yes, I'll call you in the morning.'

She replaced the receiver and stood for a moment looking down at the Bay. She must have been doing that for the last hour. There were no searchlights tonight; and no angel was clamped like an aerial frogman to the wall out there, with his animal eyes upon her and his angelic, unshaven cheek pressed close to the bricks. Only below, in the dark of the Moreton Bay figs – those exiles of her own northern shore – the flying-foxes, gorging on fruit.

She turned the lights out and went into her bedroom. Brightness and squalor of a small star's dressing-room – den of a sorceress whose spells were expert and false according to the times, and whose powers had been worked up always out of improvident energies. Well, that spring was dry. All that was left were the half-empty bottles of the witch's fakery: cut-glass in what the boys these days called Deco, plastic jars full of liquors, creams, milks, balms, emulsions – unmagic potions. Unzipping the good black dress, she hung it like an empty skin in the closet – one of the rules – then sat and rolled off her stockings, leaving them anyhow on the floor; underclothes the same – she had always been messy. 'You're impossible,' people told her, 'you're such a perfectionist.' 'No,' she had sometimes answered, bitter at being misunderstood, 'I'm a slob.' The nuns had known. 'Clay McHugh,' she heard an old nun, Sister Ignatia complain, 'if your mind in any way resembles your closet you're in for a hard time. We shall say nothing of your soul.' They had none of them said anything of her soul.

So she was naked.

She groaned aloud now, since there was no one to hear, and drew back the sheet. She lay her body out: the slack flesh of her arms and thighs, her wrinkled belly, her skull and her feet and her hands that were covered with blotches, patches of darkness that would spread.

I am lying with the goose, she told herself, that's how they'll find me. Only nobody dies of grief – grief doesn't kill us. We're too damned selfish and strong – and what we love in the end is the goose.

She unsnapped the chain. It was too heavy to sleep with. It dragged you down into dreams. With a solid clunk it hit the night-table, all her stories, her insoluble mysteries: a dead sound, *clunk*, just like that – the last sound before silence.

THE ONLY SPEAKER OF
HIS TONGUE

He has already been pointed out to me: a flabby, thickset man of fifty-five or sixty, very black, working alongside the others and in no way different from them – or so it seems. When they work he swings his pick with the same rhythm. When they pause he squats and rolls a cigarette, running his tongue along the edge of the paper while his eyes, under the stained hat, observe the straight line of the horizon; then he sets it between his lips, cups flame, draws in, and blows out smoke like all the rest.

Wears moleskins looped low under his belly and a flannel vest. Sits at smoko on one heel and sips tea from an enamel mug. Spits, and his spit hisses on stone. Then rises, spits in his palm and takes up the pick. They are digging holes for fencing-posts at the edge of the plain. When called he answers immediately, 'Here, boss,' and then, when he has approached, 'Yes boss, you wanna see me?' I am presented and he seems amused, as if I were some queer northern bird he had heard about but never till now believed in, a sort of crane perhaps, with my grey frock-coat and legs too spindly in their yellow trousers; an odd, angular fellow with yellow-grey side-whiskers, half spectacles and a cold-sore on his lip. So we stand face to face.

He is, they tell me, the one surviving speaker of his tongue. Half a century back, when he was a boy, the last of his people were massacred. The language, one of hundreds (why make a fuss?) died with them. Only not quite. For all his lifetime this man has spoken it, if only to himself. The words, the great system of sound and silence (for all languages, even the simplest, are a great and complex system) are locked up now in his heavy skull, behind the folds of the black brow (hence my scholarly interest), in the mouth with its stained teeth and fat, rather pink tongue. It is alive still in the man's silence, a whole alternative universe, since the world as we know it is in the last resort the words through which we imagine and name it; and when he narrows his eyes, and grins and says 'Yes, boss, you wanna see me?', it is not breathed out.

I am (you may know my name) a lexicographer. I come to these shores from far off, out of curiosity, a mere tourist, but in my own land I too am the keeper of something: of the great book of words of my tongue. No, not mine, my people's, which they have made over centuries, up there in our part of the world, and in which, if you have an ear for these things and a nose for the particular fragrance of a landscape, you may glimpse forests, lakes, great snow-peaks that hang over our land like the wings of birds. It is all there in our mouths. In the odd names of our villages, in the pet-names we give to pigs or cows, and to our children too when they are young, Little Bean, Pretty Cowslip; in the nonsense rhymes in which so much simple wisdom is contained (not by accident, the language itself discovers these truths), or in the way, when two consonants catch up a repeated sound, a new thought goes flashing from one side to another of your head.

All this is mystery. It is a mystery of the deep past, but also of now. We recapture on our tongue, when we first grasp the sound and make it, the same word in the mouths of our long dead fathers, whose blood we move in and whose blood still moves in us. Language *is* that blood. It is the sun taken up where it shares out heat and light to the surface of each thing and made whole, hot, round again. *Solen,* we say, and the sun stamps once on the plain and pushes up in its great hot body, trailing streams of breath.

O holiest of all holy things! – it is a stooped blond crane that tells you this, with yellow side-whiskers and the grey frockcoat and trousers of his century – since we touch here on beginnings, go deep down under Now to the remotest dark, far back in each ordinary moment of our speaking, even in gossip and the rigmarole of love words and children's games, into the lives of our fathers, to share with them the single instant of all our seeing and making, all our long history of doing and being. When I think of my tongue being no longer alive in the mouths of men a chill goes over me that is deeper than my own death, since it is the gathered death of all my kind. It is black night descending once and forever on all that world of forests, lakes, snow peaks, great birds' wings; on little fishing sloops, on foxes nosing their way into a coop, on the piles of logs that make bonfires, and the heels of the young girls leaping over them, on sewing-needles, milk pails, axes, on gingerbread moulds made out of good birchwood, on fiddles, school slates, spinning-tops – my breath catches, my heart jumps. O the holy dread of it! Of having under your tongue the first and last words of all those generations down there in your blood, down there in the earth, for whom these syllables were the magic once for calling the whole of creation to come striding, swaying, singing towards them. I look at this old fellow and my heart stops, I do not know what to say to him.

I am curious, of course – what else does it mean to be a scholar but to be curious and to have a passion for the preserving of things? I would like to have him speak a word or two in his own tongue. But the desire is frivolous, I am ashamed to ask. And in what language would I do it? This foreign one? Which I speak out of politeness because I am a visitor here, and speak well because I have learned it, and he because it is the only one he can share now with his contemporaries, with those who fill the days with him – the language (he appears to know only a handful of words) of those who feed, clothe, employ him, and whose great energy, and a certain gift for changing and doing things, has set all this land under another tongue. For the land too is in another language now. All its capes and valleys have new names; so do its creatures – even the insects that make their own skirling, racketing sound under stones. The first landscape here is dead. It dies in this man's eyes as his tongue licks the edge of the horizon, before it has quite dried up in his mouth. There is a new one now that others are making.

So. It is because I am a famous visitor, a scholarly freak from another continent, that we have been brought together. We have nothing to say to one another. I come to the fire where he sits with the rest of the men and accept a mug of their sweet scalding tea. I squat with difficulty in my yellow trousers. We nod to one another. He regards me with curiosity, with a kind of shy amusement, and sees what? Not fir forests, surely, for which he can have neither picture nor word, or lakes, snow-peaks, a white bird's wing. The sun perhaps, our northern one, making a long path back into the dark, and the print of our feet, black tracks upon it.

Nothing is said. The men are constrained by the presence of a stranger, but also perhaps by the presence of the boss. They make only the most rudimentary attempts at talk: slow monosyllabic remarks, half-swallowed with the tea. The thread of community here is strung with a few shy words and expletives – grunts, caws, soft bursts of laughter that go back before syntax; the man no more talkative than the rest, but a presence just the same.

I feel his silence. He sits here, solid, black, sipping his tea and flicking away with his left hand at a fly that returns again and again to a spot beside his mouth; looks up so level, so much on the horizontal, under the brim of his hat.

Things centre themselves upon him – that is what I feel, it is eerie – as on the one and only repository of a name they will lose if he is no longer there to keep it in mind. He holds thus, on a loose thread, the whole circle of shabby-looking trees, the bushes with their hidden life, the infinitesimal coming and going among grassroots or on ant-trails between stones, the minds of small native creatures that come creeping to the edge of the scene and look in at us from their other lives. He gives no sign of being special. When their smoking time is up, he rises with the rest, stretches a little, spits in the palm of his hand, and goes silently to his work.

'Yes boss, you wanna see me' – neither a statement nor a question, the only words I have heard him speak . . .

I must confess it. He has given me a fright. Perhaps it is only that I am cut off here from the use of my own tongue (though I have never felt such a thing on previous travels, in France, Greece, Egypt), but I find it necessary, in the privacy of my little room with its marble-topped washbasin and commodious jug and basin, and the engraving of Naomi bidding farewell to Ruth – I find it necessary, as I pace up and down on the scrubbed boards in the heat of a long December night, to go over certain words as if it were only my voice naming them in the dark that kept the loved objects solid and touchable in the light up there, on the top side of the world. (Goodness knows what sort of spells my hostess thinks I am making, or the children, who see me already as a spook, a half-comic, half-sinister wizard of the north.)

So I say softly as I curl up with the sheet over my head, or walk up and down, or stand at the window a moment before this plain that burns even at midnight: *rogn, valnøtt, spiseskje, hakke, vinglass, lysestake, krabbe, kjegle* . . .

OUT OF THE STREAM

The boy stood in the doorway and was not yet visible.

The others were at breakfast. He stood leaning against the refrigerator, which was taller than he was, a great white giant that made ice, endlessly made ice, and whose shelves (the brightest place in the house) were packed with bowls of asparagus tips, beetroot, egg-custard, roll-mops, tubs of Neapolitan gelati, cheesecake, pizzas, T-bone steaks. No one bothered to look up.

He would step out soon – but as what? A stranger from the streets, filthy from sleeping on building-sites or at the end of alleys among the rubbish-tins and piss; demanding that they take him in and feed him, or find a place for him in their beds. As a courier of the air, one of those agents of apocalypse that are forever in course about the planet, bearing news of earthquake, epidemic, famine, and the coming now of the last invaders. As an exterminating angel swinging a two-edged sword and bringing them back to the first things of all, to blood and breath. As anything but the fourteen-year-old he was, descending only from a night among the hot sheets and a room whose Cat Stevens poster (which belonged to the time when he was a Cat Stevens fan), and his dictionaries, calculator, tape-recorder and head-set – and the silhouettes of all the ships of cruiser class in the Japanese navy of forty years ago – might define the whole of his interests and what he was.

He stepped out of the lee of the white giant, in T-shirt and jeans, his hair combed wet from the shower. The two-edged sword went swinging.

'You're late,' his mother complained, without even looking to see who it was.

'It's all right,' he said. 'I don't want anything. Just tea.'

His mother poured it with her back to him, where she was preparing salads for their picnic, and he came and took it from the bench.

His father was eating toast, snapping clean rounds out of it with his teeth and devouring the *Sun*. Michael was on the floor with the comics. Only Julie, all in white for tennis, her shoulders brown and bare, was sitting up straight and eating the way people were supposed to eat; and doing it beautifully as she did everything.

She was sixteen, two years older than Luke, and did not know how extraordinary she was. Her presence among them was a mystery. It had always amazed him that they were of the same family, especially in the days before Michael when there had been just the two of them. People were always proclaiming in that silly way, 'What beautiful children!' But they had meant Julie. Any likeness between them was illusory, and when Michael appeared and was such an ugly duckling, Luke had felt easier, as if a balance was restored. He had a special fondness for Michael's bat-like ears.

'Well, are you coming out or aren't you?' his father demanded.

'No. I promised to see Hughie.'

His mother made a straight line with her mouth. Hughie was the son of the man who had made the sails for their boat. She didn't approve of that. It was all right when they were just kids at primary school, but now he was supposed to have other friends. He did not.

'But you said you would,' Michael wailed. 'You promised! I don't want to go either.'

Michael was eight and still said exactly what he felt. It embarrassed Luke that Michael was so fond of him and did not dissemble or hide it. He felt Michael's affection as a weight that he might never throw off. He hated to hurt people, and was always doing it, whichever way he turned – Michael, Julie, his mother.

'I can't,' he said again. 'I promised Hughie.'

Michael turned away and his mother gave him one of her looks of silent reproval: he was so selfish.

He had in fact made no promise to Hughie, but ten minutes later he came round the harbour path with its morning-glory vines and its wall of moss-covered, dripping rocks to where the Hutchins's house was built above the water, with a slatted ramp beside it. The walls of the house were of stained shingles, and at night you could hear water lapping below and the masts of pleasure-boats tapping and clicking.

Luke had known it always. It was a big open house full of light and air, but since Hughie's mother died, six months ago, had been let go. There were cartons in the hallway crammed with old newspapers and boating magazines that no one had bothered to move, already cobwebbed and thick with dust. In the kitchen, away to the right, flies buzzed among open jam-jars and unscraped plates where T-bones lay congealed in fat and streaks of hardened tomato sauce, a bottle of which, all black at the rim, stood open on the oilskin cloth. It was all mess – Luke didn't mind that; but beyond the mess of the two or three rooms where Hughie and his father camped, you were aware of rooms that were empty, where nobody ever went. They gave your voice in this house a kind of echo – that is what Luke thought – and made Hughie, these days, a bit weird. As if all those empty rooms were a part of him he could no longer control. 'Is that you, Luke?' he called now, and his voice had the echo. 'C'mon through.'

He was the youngest of three brothers. The eldest, Ric, was a panel-beater. He lived in the Western suburbs with a girl who was just out of school. The other had got in with a drug crowd, and after a period of hanging round the city in a headband and waistcoat, had gone to Nimbin and was raising corn. Hughie was the baby. Spoiled and petted by his mother when she was alive, he had been drifting since. He spent his days in front of the TV or up at the Junction, bare-footed in board-shorts, with the Space Invaders.

An excessively skinny kid, always tanned but still unhealthy-looking, he was sprawled now on the vinyl lounge in front of the

TV, wearing the stained blue board-shorts that he never changed and with his fist in a packet of crisps. He took his hand from the packet and crammed a fistful into his mouth, then licked the salt from his fingers before it dropped. 'Want some?' he asked through the crunching.

Luke shook his head. 'Why do you eat that stuff?'

'Because I saw it on TV,' Hughie answered straight off. 'And because I'm dumb and don't know any better. Besides, it beats ice-cubes.'

A few months back there was never anything to eat in this house except ice-cubes. They used to suck them in the heat while they watched the cricket. 'There's a choice,' Hughie would tell him, 'ice-cubes boiled or fried or grilled. Take your pick.' That was while Mrs Hutchins was still dying in the next room. 'I figure,' Hughie told him now, 'that if I eat all that stuff they eat on television – you know, potato crisps, Cherry Ripe, Coke, all that *junk,* I'll turn into a real Australian kid and have a top physique. Isn't that what's supposed to happen?'

'Maybe you'll turn into a real American kid and stay skinny.'

'Y' reckon?' Hughie's hand was arrested in mid-lift.

'Maybe you'll just get spots.'

'Nah! Nunna the kids on TV get spots. Look at 'em. They're all blond 'n have top physiques, and the girls are unreal.'

'They've got spots. That's why they use Clearasil.'

'I use Clearasil.'

'Does it do any good?'

'No, but that's because I pull off so much.'

'So do the kids on TV.'

'Y' reckon?'

He leaned out, flicked to another channel, then another, then pushed the off-switch with his big toe.

'Maybe you'll just turn into yourself,' Luke said, 'only you'll be too full of junk to see what it is.'

'But that's just what I *don't* want. You ever see anyone on TV looked like me? I wanna be a real Australian kid. You know – happy. Sliding down a water-chute with lots of other happy kids, including girls. Climbing all over a big ball and making things go better with Coke. That's why I'm into junk food. Junk food makes you tanned and gives you a terrific physique. It's pulling off gives you spots.'

'No. It doesn't do anything.'

'Yes it does. It turns you into a monster.'

Hughie jumped up, made jerking movements with his fist and turned into a pale skinny version of King Kong. He hopped about on flat feet with his knees bent, his arms loose and his tongue pushed into his upper lip, grunting. Luke jumped up, made the same motions and was Frankenstein. Laughing, they fell in a heap.

'No,' Luke said, sitting upright, 'it doesn't do any of that. They just tell you that because they can't sell it on TV.'

Hughie went back to munching crisps.

'So what'll you do?' he said, returning to a conversation of several days back.

'I don't know. What about you?'

'My dad says I can leave school if I want to and go in with him. There's a lot of money in sailmaking. You know?' He said it without enthusiasm. 'Everyone wants sails.'

'I want to do Japanese,' Luke said, moving to the window and looking across to the marina, where half a mile off, among a crowd of Sunday craft, he could see *Starlight* just beginning to make way. He was thinking of a time, a year back, when with his grandfather as guide he would go crawling about in the strange light of the sea off Midway, among the wrecks of the Japanese carriers *Soryu, Kaga, Hiryu*, Admiral Nagumo's flagship the *Akagi*, the heavy cruiser *Mikuma*, and the *Yorktown*. 'My Grandad says we might have been better off,' he said reflectively, 'if we hadn't won the Battle of Midway after all and the Japs had come instead of the Americans. I don't know, maybe he's right. He says winning all those wars was the worst thing ever happened to us.'

'Is this your grandfather who was in the Wehrmacht?' Hughie enquired.

Luke giggled. 'No, you nut! They lost all *their* wars. My Dad's father. The one who was in the AIF.'

Hughie, still hugging the carton of crisps, got up and went to the other side of the room.

'Listen Luke,' he said seriously, 'I've been meaning to tell you. If you need any money I've got stacks of it.'

'What?'

'Money. Com'n look.'

He was standing over an open drawer.

'My Dad's got this woman he goes to, and every time he goes off and leaves me alone I get ten dollars. I mean, he *gives* it to me. I'm making a fortune!' The two boys stood looking at the drawer full of bills. 'He feels guilty, see? I ran into them once, up at the Junction, and they were both so embarrassed. She's a sort of barmaid. I had to stop myself from laughing. I feel like I'm living off her immoral earnings, ten dollars a time. If you want any of it, it's yours.'

Luke looked at the drawer and shook his head. 'No,' he said, 'I get pocket money, they give me pocket money. Anyway, all I need now is ninety-five cents for the train fare.'

'I dunno,' Hughie said before the open drawer. 'Why does 'e do it? What's 'e scared of?' He looked sad standing there in the board-shorts, so buck-toothed and skinny, peering into the drawer full of bills. They had called him Casper at school. Casper the ghost.

'My parents,' Luke said, 'are scared of all sorts of things.' And at first to take Hughie's mind off his problem, but soon out of a growing contempt and bitterness of his own, he began to list them. 'They're scared one of us will go on drugs or join the Jesus freaks or the Hari Krishnas. Or grow up and marry a Catholic. My mother's scared of being poor, the way they were in Europe after the war. She's scared my father's dad'll get sick and have to come and live with us. She's scared of cancer. My Dad's scared the tax people will catch up with him.' He turned away to the window, and *Starlight* was just moving down towards the point opposite. He could see his father amidships, in his captain's cap, directing: 'There's only one captain on this boat,' he would be saying. 'Most of all,' Luke said, 'he's scared of my mother. He thinks he's not good enough for her.' At the prow was Michael, a lonely child, dangling his legs on either side of the bowsprit. Luke could see one dazzling white sneaker.

'Listen, I'll tell you what,' he said, 'why don't we go out and fly the kites? We haven't done that for ages.'

'You really want to?'

'Yes, it's *just* what I want.' He hadn't thought of it till this moment but it was true. 'It's what I came for.'

Last year when they had both seemed so much younger they had spent hours flying the kites, two big box-kites that Hughie's father had made with the same craftsman's skill he brought to his sail-making. They were beautiful machines, and for a while Luke had liked nothing better than to be at the end of a string and to feel the gentle tugging of the birdlike creation that was three-hundred feet up under the ceiling of cloud and gently afloat, or plunging in the breeze – feeling it as another freer self, almost angelic, and with a will of its own. No other activity he knew gave him such a clear sense of being both inside his own compact body and far outside it. You strained, you held on, the plunging was elsewhere.

Hughie was delighted to drag the kites out of the back room where they had been gathering dust for the past months and to check and re-wind the strings. He did it quickly but with great concentration. He tied the sleeves of a light sweater round his waist and they were off.

Twenty minutes later the kites with their gaudy tails were sailing high over the rocky little park on the Point and far out over the water. Luke too had removed his shirt and was running over the grass, feeling the kite tug him skyward: *tug, tug.* He could feel the sky currents up there, the pure air in motion, feel its energy run all the way back along the string into his gorged hands. It took him to the limits of his young strength.

'This is great,' Hughie was shouting as if they had suddenly stepped back a year. 'Feel that? Isn't it unreal?'

They let their animal selves loose and the great kites held and sustained them.

'What really shits me,' Luke said later when they had drawn the machines in, wound the strings and were lying stretched in the shade, 'is that no one has the guts to be what they pretend to be. You know what I mean? My father pretends to be a big businessman. He makes deals and talks big but it scares hell out of him, and at the weekend he pretends to be the skipper of a boat. He gets all dressed up in his whites and does a lot of shouting but all the time he's terrified a storm'll blow up or he'll ram someone or that Michael will fall in and get drowned. People are all the same. You can see it. Scared you'll call their bluff. It makes me puke.'

Hughie looked puzzled. Luke worried him. Most of the time he was just like anyone, the way he was when they were flying the kites: then suddenly he'd speak out, and there was more anger in what he said than the words themselves could contain.

'So?' he said.

'So someone, sometime, has to go through with it.'

'How do you mean?'

Luke set his mouth and did not elaborate, and Hughie, out of loyalty to an old understanding between them, did not push for an answer.

They had known one another since they were five or six years old. It was, in terms of their short lives, a long friendship, but Hughie had begun to perceive lately, and it hurt him, that they might already have grown apart. There was in Luke something dark, uncompromising, fanatical, that scared him because it was so alien to his own nature. He was incapable of such savagery himself, and might be the shallower for it. His mind struggled to grasp the thing and it hurt.

'Listen Luke,' he began, then stopped and was defeated. There was no way of putting what he had seen into words. He swallowed, picked at his toe. Luke, hard-mouthed and with brows fiercely lowered, was staring dead ahead. 'Hey, Luke,' he called across the narrow space between them, and knocked the other boy's shoulder, very lightly, with the heel of his hand.

'What?'

'I don't know, you seemed – far away.' He screwed his eyes up and looked out across the burnished water. The idea of distance saddened him.

'Thanks,' Luke said softly after a moment, and Hughie was relieved.

'For what?' he answered, but it wasn't a question.

They grinned, and it was as if things between them were clear again. Luke got up. 'I'd better get going,' he said. 'I'll give you a hand with the kites.'

Two hours later he was getting down at the empty northern station with its cyclone-wire fence strung on weathered uprights. The view beyond was of the sea.

He made his way along a tussocky path that led away from the main settlement, and along the edge of the dunes to where his grandfather's shack, grey fibro, stood in a fenceless allotment above rocks. There were banksias all leaning one way, shaped by the wind and rattling their dry, grey-black cones. It was a desolate place, not yet tamed or suburban: the dunes held together by long silvery grass, changing their contours almost daily under the wind; the sea-light harsh, almost brutal, stinging your eyes, blasting the whole world white with salt. Inland, to the west, great platforms of sandstone held rainwater in rusty pools and the wild bush-plants, spiky green now but when they were in flower a brilliant white, thrust clean through rock.

His grandfather was a fisherman. It was his grandfather who had led Luke to the sea; and his grandfather's war (or rather the Occupation Forces of the years afterward) that had led him, through yarns quietly told and a collection of objects too deeply revered to be souvenirs – touchstones rather – to his consuming interest of this last couple of years. He had touched every one of those objects, and they had yielded their mystery. He had listened to his grandfather, read everything he could lay his hands on, and had, he thought, understood. He felt now for the key, on a hook by the water tank, and let himself in.

A shack, not a house, but orderly and to Luke's eyes, beautiful. Washing-up was stacked on the primitive sink. There was a note on the kitchen table: 'Luke – be back around five. Love, Pa.' Luke studied it. He took a glass of water, but only wet his lips, and went through to the one large room that made up the rest of the place.

It was very bare. Poor-looking, some would have thought. Everything was out and visible: straw mats of a pale corn colour, still with a smell; his grandfather's stretcher; the hammock where Luke himself slept when he stayed overnight. On the walls, the table-top, and on the floor round the walls, were the objects that made this for Luke a kind of shrine: masks, pots, the two samurai swords and daggers.

He went straight to the wall and took one of the daggers from its hook – it was his, and walking through to the open verandah, he stood holding it a moment, then drew the sharp blade from its sheath.

He ran his finger along the edge, not drawing blood, then, barely thinking, turned the point towards him and made a hard jab with his fist. It was arrested just at the white of his T-shirt.

He gave a kind of laugh. It would be so easy. You would let each thing happen, one thing after the next, in an order that once established would carry you right through and over into –

He stood very still, letting it begin.

At the moment of his first stepping in across the threshold out of the acute sunlight, he had entered a state – he couldn't have said what it was, but had felt the strangeness of it like a trance upon his blood, in which everything moved slowly, slowly. He was not dulled – not at all – but he felt out of himself, free of his own being, or aware of it in a different way. It came to him, this new being of his, as a clear fact like the dagger; like the light off the walls, which was reflected sea-light blasting the fibro with a million tumbling particles; like the individual dry strands of the matting.

You fell into such states, anyway he did, but not always so deeply. They began in strangeness and melancholy – you very nearly vanished – then when you came back, it was to a sense of the oneness of things. There was a kind of order in the world and it was in you as well. You attended. You caught a rhythm to which each gesture could be fitted. You let it lead you out of your body into –

It had begun. Slowly he removed his watch – it was twelve past four – and laid it on a ledge. Then he took off his gym shoes, pushed his socks into them and set them side by side on the floor. He pulled his T-shirt over his head and, folding his jeans, made a pile of them, jeans, T-shirt, shoes. They looked like the clothes, neatly arranged, of one who had gone into the sea or into the air – how could you be certain which? – or into the earth. The sea was glittering on his left and was immense. He did not look at it. Earth and air you took for granted. Wearing only the clean jockey-shorts now, he knelt on the verandah boards, carefully arranging his limbs: bringing his body into a perpendicular line with his foot soles, and thighs and trunk into alignment with the dagger, which lay immediately before him. He sat very straight, his body all verticals, horizontals, strictly composed; in a straight line with sea and earth, or at right angles to them. He began to breathe in and out, deeply, slowly, feeling the oxygen force its way into his cells so that they exerted a pressure all over the surface of him where his body met the air, in the beginning muscles of his forearms and biceps, in his throat, his lips, against the thinness of his closed lids. He clenched his teeth, the breath in his nostrils now a steady hiss, and took up the dagger. All there was now was the business of getting the body through and over into –

He paused. He set the point of the dagger to the skin of belly above the white jockey-shorts (death was so close – as close as that) and all the muscles of his abdomen fluttered at the contact. He felt his sex begin to stiffen, all of itself.

A wave, not very big, had begun making for the shore and would reach it soon with a scuffling of pebbles, one of which, the one in his mouth, had a taste of salt. He sucked on it, and over a long period, after centuries, it began to be worn away, it melted, and his mouth, locked on the coming cry, was filled with the words of a new language, on his tongue, his tooth ridge, as a gurgling in his throat: the names of ordinary objects – tools, cookpots, baskets – odd phrases or conversations on which a life might depend, jokes (even crude ones), lyrics praising the moon or lilies or the rising of a woman's breast, savage epics –

'That you, Luke?'

The boy came back into himself, the wave passed on. He opened his eyes, picked up the sheath, pushed himself to his feet, and with dagger and sheath still in hand, walked barefoot, and naked save for his jockeys, to the door.

His grandfather was there. He had a heavy sack over his shoulder and a rod and reel.

'Hullo Luke,' he called. He swung the sack down hard on the concrete path. 'I had a good day,' he said. He gave a crack-lipped grin. 'Take a look at this.' He lifted the end of the sack, tumbling its contents in a cascade of shining bodies. Luke was dazzled. Some of them were still alive and flipping their tails on the rough concrete, throwing light.

The boy restored the dagger to its sheath, rested it on the edge of the sink, and stepped down among them. 'Terrific,' he said.

'Yairs,' the man breathed, 'pretty good, eh? You stoppin' the night?'

Luke nodded, moving quickly away to catch a fish that was flapping off into the coarse grass. It continued to flutter in his hands.

'Good,' said the man. He went off to fetch buckets and knives. 'We'll get started, eh?'

While his grandfather went through into the kitchen to get clean basins, Luke took one of the buckets round to the side of the house and filled it from the tank. He came back staggering.

'Good,' his grandfather said. 'Let's get into it.'

They seated themselves side by side on the step and worked swiftly.

It was a job Luke was used to, had been skilled at since he was nine years old. The blade went in along the belly; the guts spilled, a lustrous silver-blue, and were tossed into the one bucket; in the other you plunged to the forearm and rinsed.

The work went on quickly, silently; they seldom talked much till after tea. Luke lost himself in the rhythm of it, a different rhythm from the one he had given himself to earlier. A kind of drowsiness came over him, that had to do with the falling darkness, with the repeated flashing of the knife and his swinging to left and right between buckets, and with the closeness of so much raw flesh and blood. His arms and bare legs were covered with fish-scales. His face, neck, chest were flecked with gobbets of the thin fish blood.

At last they were done. The fish, all scaled and gutted, were in the basins. One bucket was full of guts, the other with water that was mostly blood. The doorstep too was all shiny with scales (Luke would come out later and flush it clean).

'Good,' his grandfather said. 'We've done well.' He carried in the basins of fish, then took the two heavy buckets and poured them into a dip in the sand where they could be covered. Luke sat, too drowsy to move; but stirred himself at last. He went round to the side of the house and let water run over his legs, and washed the scales from his neck and arms.

It was almost dark. You could hear the sea washing against the rocks below, a regular crashing; but further out it was still, and he stood a moment, clean again, drying off in the breeze, and watched it. He felt oddly happy – for no reason, there *was* no reason. Just happy, as earlier with the kites. It was like a change of weather, a sudden transformation, that might not last but for as long as it did would fill the whole sky and touch everything around with its steady light. He was back in the stream again – one of the streams.

He went in and began to dress: jeans (not caring that he was still half wet), T-shirt. His grandfather was frying fish for their tea. The fish smelled good and he was hungry.

'Set the table, Luke,' his grandfather told him. 'She'll be ready in a jiff.'

So he set the two places at the kitchen table, then stood for a moment at the open door and looked out into the dark. It seemed larger, more comprehensible, because it lay over the sea and you saw it as an ocean whose name you knew and knew the other shore of, glittering full under the early stars; though the dark was bigger than any ocean, bigger even than the sky with its scattered lights.

'Right,' the old man called. 'We're all set, Luke. You hungry?'

The boy turned back to the lighted table. His grandfather, humming a little, was just setting down the pan.

THE SUN IN WINTER

It was dark in the church, even at noon. Diagonals of chill sunlight were stacked between the piers, sifting down luminous dust, and so thick with it that they seemed more substantial almost than stone. He had a sense of two churches, one raised vertically on gothic arches and a thousand years old, the other compounded of light and dust, at an angle to the first and newly created in the moment of his looking. At the end of the nave, set far back on a platform, like a miraculous vision that the arctic air had immediately snap-frozen, was a Virgin with a child at her knee. The Michael-angelo. So this church he was in must be the Onze Vrouw.

'Excuse me.'

The voice came from a pew two rows away, behind him: a plain woman of maybe forty, with the stolid look and close-pored waxy skin of those wives of donors he had been looking at earlier in the side panels of local altars. She was buttoned to the neck in a square-shouldered raincoat and wore a scarf rather than a wimple, but behind her as she knelt might have been two or three miniatures of herself – infant daughters with their hands strictly clasped – and if he peeped under her shoes, he thought, there would be a monster of the deep, a sad-eyed amorphous creature with a hump to its back, gloomily committed to evil but sick with love for the world it glimpsed, all angels, beyond the hem of her skirt.

'You're not Flemish, are you,' she was saying, half in question (that was her politeness) and half as fact.

'No,' he admitted. 'Australian.'

They were whispering – this was after all a church – but her 'Ah,

86

the *New* World' was no more than a breath. She made it sound so romantic, so much more of a venture than he had ever seen it, that he laughed outright, then checked himself; but not before his laughter came back to him, oddly transformed, from the hollow vault. No Australian in those days thought of himself as coming under so grand a term. Things are different now.

'You see,' she told him in a delighted whisper, 'I guessed! I knew you were not Flemish – that, if you don't mind, is obvious – so I thought, I'll speak to him in English, or maybe on this occasion I'll try Esperanto. Do you by any chance know Esperanto?' He shook his head. 'Well, never mind,' she said, 'there's plenty of time.' She did not say for what. 'But you *are* Catholic.'

Wrong again. Well, not exactly, but his 'No' was emphatic, she was taken aback. She refrained from putting the further question and looked for a moment as if she did not know how to proceed. Then following the turn of his head she found the Madonna. 'Ah,' she said, 'you are interested in art. You have come for the Madonna.' Relieved at last to have comprehended him she regarded the figure with a proprietary air. Silently, and with a certain old world grandeur and largesse, she presented it to him.

He should, to be honest, have informed her then that he had been a Catholic once (he was just twenty) and still wasn't so far gone as to be lapsed – though too far to claim communion; and that for today he had rather exhausted his interest in art at the little hospital full of Memlings and over their splendid van Eycks. Which left no reason for his being here but the crude one: his need to find sanctuary for a time from their killing cold.

Out there, blades of ice slicing in off the North Sea had found no obstacle, it seemed, in more than twenty miles of flat lands crawling with fog, till they found *him*, the one vertical (given a belltower or two) on the whole ring of the horizon. He had been, for long minutes out there, the assembly-point for forty-seven demons. His bones scraped like glaciers. Huge ice-plates ground in his skull. He had been afraid his eyeballs might freeze, contract, drop out, and go rolling away over the ancient flags. It seemed foolish after all that to say simply, 'I was cold.'

'Well, in that case,' she told him, 'you must allow me to make an appointment. I am an official guide of this town. I am working all day in a government office, motor-vehicle licences, but precisely at four we can meet and I will show you our dear sad Bruges – that is, of course, if you are agreeable. No, no – please – it is for my own pleasure, no fee is involved. Because I see that you are interested, I glimpsed it right off.' She turned up the collar of her coat and gave him an engaging smile. 'It is OK?' She produced the Americanism with a cluck of clear self-satisfaction, as proof that she was, though a guide of this old and impressively dead city, very much of his own century and not at all hoity-toity about the usages of the New World. It was a brief kick of the heels that promised fun as well as instruction in the splendours and miseries of the place.

'Well then,' she said when he made no protest, 'it is decided – till four. You will see that our Bruges is very beautiful, very *triste,* you understand French? *Bruges la Morte.* And German too maybe, a little? *Die tote Stadt.*' She pronounced this with a small shiver in her voice, a kind of silvery chill that made him think of the backs of mirrors. At the same time she gave him just the tips of her gloved fingers. 'So – I must be off now. We meet at four.'

Which is how, without especially wanting it, he came to know the whole history of the town. On a cold afternoon in the Fifties, with fog swirling thick white in the polled avenues and lying in ghostly drifts above the canals, and the red-brick façades of palaces, convents, museums laid bare under the claws of ivy, he tramped with his guide over little humpbacked bridges, across sodden lawns, to see a window the size of a hand-mirror with a bloody history, a group of torture instruments (themselves twisted now and flaking rust), the site, almost too ordinary, of a minor miracle, a courtyard where five old ladies were making lace with fingers as knobbled and misshapen as twigs, and the statue of a man in a frock coat who had given birth to the decimal system.

The woman's story he caught in the gaps between centuries and he got the two histories, her own and the city's, rather mixed, so that he could not recall later whether it was his lady or the daughter of a local duke who had suffered a fall in the woods, and her young man or some earlier one who had been shut up and tortured in one of the many towers. The building she pointed to as being the former Gestapo headquarters looked much like all the rest, though it might of course have been a late imitation.

She made light of things, including her own life, which had not, he gathered, been happy; but she could be serious as well as ironic. To see what all this really was, she insisted – beyond the relics and the old-fashioned horrors and shows – you needed a passion for the everyday. That was how she put it. And for that, mere looking got you nowhere. 'All you see then,' she told him, 'is what catches the eye, the odd thing, the unusual. But to see what is common, that is the difficult thing, don't you think? For that we need imagination, and there is never enough of it – never, never enough.'

She had spoken with feeling, and now that it was over, her own small show, there was an awkwardness. It had grown dark. The night, a block of solid ice with herrings in it, deep blue, was being cranked down over the plain; you could hear it creaking. He stamped a little, puffing clouds of white, and shyly, sheepishly grinned. 'Cold,' he sang, shuffling his feet, and when she laughed at the little dance he was doing he continued it, waving his arms about as well. Then they came, rather too quickly, to the end of his small show. She pulled at her gloves and stood waiting.

Something more was expected of him, he knew that. But what? Was he to name it? Should he perhaps, in spite of her earlier disclaimer, offer a tip? Was that it? Surely not. But money was just one of the things, here in Europe, that he hadn't got the hang of, the weight, the place, the meaning; one of the many – along with tones, looks, little movements of the hands and eyebrows, unspoken demands and the easy meeting of them – that more than galleries or torture chambers made up what he had come here to see, and to absorb too if he could manage it. He felt hopelessly young and raw. He ought to have known – he had known – from that invisible kick of the heels, that she had more to show him than this crumblingly haunted and picturesque corner of the past, where sadness, a mood of silvery reflection, had been turned into the high worship of death – a glory perhaps, but one that was too full of shadows to bear the sun. He felt suddenly a great wish for the sun in its full power as at home, and it burned up in him. He *was* the sun. It belonged to the world he had come from and to his youth.

The woman had taken his hand. 'My dear friend,' she was saying, with that soft tremor in her voice, ' – I *can* call you that, can't I? I feel that we *are* friends. In such a short time we have grown close. I would like to show you one thing more – very beautiful but not of the past. Something personal.'

She led him along the edge of the canal and out into a street broader than the rest, its cobbles gleaming in the mist. Stone steps led up to classical porticoes, and in long, brightly-lit windows there were Christmas decorations, holly with red ribbons, and bells powdered with frost. They came to a halt in front of one of the largest and brightest of these displays, and he wondered why. Still at the antipodes, deep in his dream of sunlight and youth, he did not see at first that they had arrived.

'There,' the woman was saying. She put her nose to the glass and there was a ring of fog.

The window was full of funerary objects: ornamental wreaths in iridescent enamel, candles of all sizes like organ-pipes in carved and coloured wax, angels large and small, some in glass, some in plaster, some in honey-coloured wood in which you saw all the decades of growth; one of them was playing a lute; others had viols, pan pipes, primitive sidedrums; others again pointed a slender index finger as at a naughty child and were smiling in an ambiguous, un-otherworldly way. It was all so lively and colourful that he might have missed its meaning altogether without the coffin, which held a central place in the foreground and was tilted so that you saw the richness of the buttoned interior. Very comfortable it looked too – luxuriously inviting. Though the scene did not suggest repose. The heavy lid had been pushed strongly aside, as if what lay there just a moment ago had got up, shaken itself after long sleep, and gone striding off down the quay. The whole thing puzzled him. He wondered for a moment if she hadn't led him to the site of another and more recent miracle. But no.

'Such a coffin,' she was telling him softly, 'I have ordered for myself. – Oh, don't look surprised! – I am not planning to die so soon, not at all! I am paying it off. The same. Exactly.'

He swallowed, nodded, smiled, but was dismayed; he couldn't have been more so, or felt more exposed and naked, if she had climbed up into the window, among the plump and knowing angels, and got into the thing – lain right down on the buttoned blue satin, and with her skirt rucked up to show stockings rolled tight over snowy thighs, had crooked a finger and beckoned him with a leer to join her. He blushed for the grossness of the vision, which was all his own.

But his moment of incomprehension passed. His shock, he saw, was for an impropriety she took quite for granted and for an event that belonged, as she calmly surveyed it, to a world of exuberant and even vulgar life. The window was the brightest thing she had shown him, the brightest thing he had seen all day, the most lively, least doleful.

So he survived the experience. They both did. And he was glad to recall years after, that when she smiled and touched his hand in token of their secret sympathy, a kind of grace had come over him and he did not start as he might have done; he was relieved of awkwardness, and was moved, for all his raw youth, by an emotion he could not have named, not then – for her, but also for himself – and which he would catch up with only later, when sufficient time had passed to make them of an age.

As they already were for a second, before she let him go, and in a burst of whitened breath, said 'Now my dear, dear friend, I will exact my fee. You may buy me a cup of chocolate at one of our excellent cafés. OK?'

BAD BLOOD

Odd the conjunctions, some of them closer than any planet, that govern a life. I am an only child because of my father's brother, Uncle Jake. In an otherwise exemplary line of seven brothers and sisters he made so sharp a detour, and so alarmed my mother with the statistical possibilities, that she refused, once my father's desire for an heir had been satisfied, to take further risks. She was not, needless to say, a gambler – even one chance was one too many – and she spent a good deal of her time watching for signs of delinquency in me. As the years passed and familiar features began to emerge, a nose from one side of the family, a tendency to bronchitis from the other, she grew more and more apprehensive, and was only mildly relieved when I came to resemble the plainest of her sisters.

A nose is obvious enough, it declares itself. So does a tendency to wheeze when the skies grow damp. But bad blood is a different matter. It takes a thousand forms and loves to disguise itself in meek and insidious qualities that allay suspicion and then endlessly and teasingly provoke it. My mother could never be sure of me. I was too quiet – it was unnatural. And Uncle Jake did leave his mark.

Was he really so bad?

Bad is hard to define. I am speaking of a time, the middle Thirties, and a place, Brisbane, in which it took very little in the way of divergence from the moderately acceptable for heads to come together and for a young person to get a reputation – and all reputations, of course, were bad.

There are crimes that defy judgment because they defy understanding. A mild-mannered newsagent shuts his shop one evening, goes out to the woodpile where chooks are dealt with, takes an axe, sits for ten minutes or so listening to the sounds of the warm suburban night, then goes in and butchers his whole family, along with a child from next door who has come in for the serials. The law-courts do what they can, and so too, at a level where local history becomes folk-lore, do the newspapers; but horrors of this sort cannot be gathered back into the web of daily living, there is too much blood, too much darkness in them. We must assume the irruption among us of some other agency, a wild-haired fury that sets its hand on a man and shakes the daylights out of him, or a god in whom the rival aspects of creation and chaos are of equal importance and who knows no rule. But bad is civil; it is small-scale, commonplace − something the good citizen, under other circumstances, might himself have done and is qualified to condemn.

'Shadily genteel' is how a famous visitor once described our city, and she was not referring, I think, to its quaint weatherboard houses with their verandahs of iron lace or to the hoop-pines and glossy native figs that make it so richly, even oppressively green.

Brisbane is a city of strict conventions and many churches, but subtropical, steamy. Shoes in a cupboard grow mould in the wet months, and on the quiet surface of things there are bubbles that explode in the heat and give off odours of corruption; everything softens and rots. There are billiard-saloons and pubs where illegal bets can be laid on all the local and southern races, and there were, not long ago, houses in Margaret and Albert Streets in the City, and at Nott Street South Brisbane, that were tolerated by the civil authorities and patronized by a good part of the male population but which remained for all ordinary purposes unmentionable − and given the corrugated-iron walls with which they were surrounded, very nearly invisible as well. Brisbane is full of shabby institutions that society turns its gaze from, and in a good many of them my Uncle Jake was known to have a hand. Always flush with money and nattily dressed, he rode to the races in a Black and White cab with his friend Hector Grierley, and could be seen on Saturday nights at the Grand Central, blowing his winnings in the company of ladies who smoked in public, painted their toenails and wore silk. Uncle Jake wore his Akubra at an unserious angle and had a taste for two-toned shoes. Loud is what people called him, but I knew him only in his quieter moments.

He liked to come around while my mother was ironing, and would stand for long hours telling her stories, trying to impress her (she was never impressed) and seeking her womanly advice.

She gave him the advice and he did not take it. It always ran clear against his nature, or interfered, just at the moment, with some scheme he had in hand. My mother made a face that said 'See, I knew it – why did you ask?'

She didn't dislike Uncle Jake. Quite the contrary. But she was afraid of his influence and she resented his idleness, his charm, his showy clothes, and the demands he made on my father. The youngest of my grandmother's children, he was also, for all the sorrow he had caused, her favourite, and it was the bad example, which even my father followed, of forgiving him every delinquency in the light of his plain good nature that my mother deplored. It seemed monstrous to her that on at least one occasion, when the police were involved, my steady, law-abiding father had had to go to a politician, and the politician to an inspector of police, to save Uncle Jake from his just deserts.

It hadn't always been so. As a very young man he had been an apprentice pastrycook. His paleness, the white cap and apron he wore, and the dusting of flour on his bare arms, had given him the look of a modest youth with a trade whose very domestic associations made him harmless or tame. He was cheeky, that's all; a good-natured fellow who liked a drink or two and was full of animal spirits, but in no way dangerous. He deceived several girls that way and some married women as well, and got the first of his reputations.

But people ignored it. He was so likeable, so full of fun, such a ready spender, and so ready as well to share his adventures in the stories he told, which were all old jokes remade and brought back into the realm of actuality. Then, at not much more than twenty, he fell in love. The girl was called Alice – she was two years older – and with rather a sheepish look before his mates (he was, after all, betraying the spirit of his own stories) he married her.

The girl's beauty made a great impression on everyone. She had the creamy blonde look that appealed to people in those days – big green eyes, a thinned-out arch of eyebrow, hair that hugged her head in a close cap then broke in tight little curls. Uncle Jake was crazy about her. He worked at the hot ovens all night and brought home from the bakery each morning a packet of fresh breakfast rolls that they ate in bed, and he made her cakes as well in the shape of frogs with open mouths, and piglets and hedgehogs. They were happy for a time, only they didn't know how to manage. The girl couldn't cook or sew and was reluctant to do housework, and Uncle Jake was ashamed to be found so often with his sleeves rolled up, washing dishes at the sink. He had always, himself, been such a clean fellow, such a neat and careful dresser. He couldn't bear dirt. They had house after house, moving on when the mess got too much for them.

They had a child as well, a little girl just like the mother, and Alice didn't know how to look after the baby either. She didn't change its nappies or keep it clean. It was always hungry, dirty, crawling about the unswept floor covered with flies. Uncle Jake was distracted. At last he stopped going to work – there were no more fresh little rolls, no more green iced frogs with open mouths. He stayed home to care for the child, while Alice, as lazy and beautiful as ever, just sat about reading *Photoplay* till he lost his temper and blacked her eye. Uncle Jake doted on the child but felt dismayed, un-manned. He fretted for his old life of careless independence.

Things went from bad to worse and when the little girl got whooping cough and died it was all over. Uncle Jake was so wild with grief that Alice had to be got out of the house, he might have killed her. She went to her mother's and never came back, and was, in my childhood, a big, blonde woman, even-tempered and fattish, who drank too much.

As for Uncle Jake, he recovered his spirits at last, but he never went back to the bakery or to any settled life. He had had his taste of that. Nobody blamed Alice for what had happened to him. He had simply, people said, reverted to his original wildness, which the apprenticeship to flour and icing-sugar, and his diversion for a time into suburban marriage, had done nothing to change.

All this had happened long before I was born. By the time of my earliest childhood Uncle Jake was already a gambler. It was the period of his flash suits, his brushes with the law, and the little orange car.

This beautiful machine, quite the grandest present I ever received, was his gift for my fourth birthday. 'There,' he exulted when we all trooped out to the verandah to look, 'it's for the kid.' It sat on the front lawn in its cellophane wrappers like a miniature Trojan Horse.

My father was embarrassed: partly at being so ostentatiously outdone (my parents' present had been a cricket bat and ball), but also because he was fond of my uncle, knew how generous he could be, and was certain that my mother would disapprove.

She did. She regarded the machine, all gleaming and flame-coloured, as an instrument of the devil. Whenever I rode in it, furiously working the pedals and making a *hrummm hrumm hrummm* sound as I hurtled round the yard, she would look pained and beg me after a time to spare her head. The little orange car brought out a recklessness in me, a passion for noise and speed, that appalled her. I had always been such a quiet little boy. Was this it? Was this the beginning of it? Just working my legs so fast to get the wheels going introduced me to realms of sweaty excitement I couldn't have imagined till now – to scope, to risk! I had discovered at last the power that was coiled in my own small body, the depth of my lungs, the extraordinary joys of speed and dirt and accidents – of actually spilling and grazing a knee. Uncle Jake was beside himself. He had thought of me till then as a bit of a sissy, but look at this! 'He's a real little tiger,' he said admiringly. 'Just look at him go!'

Uncle Jake was too attractive. My mother tried to keep him away but it wasn't possible. He was family. He was always there.

I remember catching my parents once in a rare but heated quarrel. There was a family wedding or funeral to attend and the question had arisen of who might look after me.

'No,' my mother whispered, 'he's irresponsible. I won't have the child traipsing around billiard-saloons or sitting in gutters outside hotels. Or riding in a cab with that Hector Grierley. He's an abortionist! Everyone knows it.'

'He could spend the day at Ruby's.'

I heard my mother gasp.

'Have you gone off your head?'

Ruby was one of Uncle Jake's girlfriends, a big china-doll of a woman who lived with her daughters at Stones Corner.

What my mother did not know was that I had been to Ruby's already. Uncle Jake and I had dropped in there for an hour or so after an outing, and I had been impressed by his insistence that I swear, scout's honour, not to let on. The act of swearing and the establishment of complicity between us had made me see the quite ordinary house, which was on high stumps with a single hallway from front to back, in a special light.

Ruby wore pink fur slippers and was sitting when we arrived on the front doorstep, painting soft, mustard-yellow wax on her legs, which she then drew off like sticking plaster, in strips. She had a walnut-veneer cocktail cabinet, and even at three in the afternoon it came brilliantly alight when you opened the doors. I was allowed, along with the two skinny daughters, to sip beer with lemonade in it; and later, while Uncle Jake and Ruby had a little lie down, I went off with the two girls, and a setter with a tail that swept the air like a scarlet feather, to see their under-the-house.

'Watch out for the dead marines, love,' Ruby had called after us in her jolly voice, and one of the daughters, giggling at my puzzlement, indicated the stack of Fourex bottles on the back landing. 'She means *them,* you dill!'

Among the objects that had taken my eye at Ruby's was a bowl of roses, perfect buds and open blooms in red, yellow, and pink, that looked supernaturally real but were not. I had never seen anything so teasingly beautiful, and when I left, one of the scarlet buds went with me. In crossing the hallway on my way to the toilet I had stopped, unhooked the most brilliant of them from its wire basket, and taking advantage of my time behind the bathroom door, had slipped it easily into my pants.

'Ruby's,' my mother said firmly, 'is out of the question. I'm surprised at you even suggesting it.'

So with Ruby's hotly in mind, and exaggerated in retrospect as a carnival place of forbidden colour, I spent the day with a neighbour, Mrs Chard, who took me on a tram-ride to the Dutton Park terminus, questioned me closely about Jesus, and informed me that she was descended from Irish kings, 'though you mightn' think it'. (I didn't, but at nearly seven was too polite to say so.) She had a place above her lip where she shaved – you could see the shadow picked out in sweat drops – and seemed quite unaware of how the afternoon in her company was transfigured by the pink glow of my imagination, and how her louvred weatherboard became for a moment, as we approached it, the site of lurid possibilities – not perhaps a cocktail cabinet, but some equally exotic object that would be continuous with the world of Ruby's where it had been decided I should *not* spend the day.

But there was nothing. Only the smell of bacon fat in the kitchen, that clogged the back of my throat the way it clogged the drains, and an upright with candleholders.

Mrs Chard played something classical in which she crossed her plump, freckled wrists; then 'Mother McCrea'. After which she showed me photographs, all of children who were dead. Then, acting on some compulsion of her own, or responding perhaps to a mood that I myself had created, she disappeared into a room across the hallway and came back holding her hands behind her back and looking very coy and knowing.

I was fascinated. She hadn't seemed at all like a woman who could tempt.

Suddenly, with a little cry and a not-quite-pleasant giggle, she produced from behind her back a pair of glossy dancing-shoes such as little girls in those days wore to tap-dancing classes, and waggled them seductively before me. They were Kelly green, and were too small for her hands, which she was using to make them dance soundlessly on the air. Uncertain how to react, I smiled, and Mrs Chard fell to her knees.

She set the Kelly green shoes on the linoleum, where they sat empty and flat; then shuffling forward, she lifted me up, set me on the piano stool, and while I watched in a trancelike state of pure astonishment, she removed my good brown shoes, took up the Kelly greens, and forced my left foot – was she mad? – into the right one and my right into the even tighter left. Then she rose up, breathy with emotion, and set me down. I stood for what seemed ages among the bone china and maidenhair in an agony of humiliation, but unable, despite every encouragement, to make the shoes take flight and release their magic syncopations.

I refused to cry. Boys do not. But Mrs Chard did. She hugged and kissed me and called me her darling, while I quailed in terror at so much emotion that both did and did not involve me; then quietened at last to heaving sobs, she fell to her knees again, snatched the shoes off, and left me to resume my own.

After our fit of shared passion she seemed unwilling to face me. When she did she was as cool as a schoolmistress. She stood watching me sweat over the laces, fixing me with a look of such plain hostility that I thought she might at any moment reach for a strap. The tap-shoes had disappeared, and it was clear to me that if I were ever to mention them, here or elsewhere, she would call me a liar and deny they had ever been.

Of course all my mother's predictions, in Uncle Jake's case, came true. He did go to gaol, though only for a month, and as he got older his charm wore off and the flash suits lost their style. The days of Cagney and George Raft gave way to years of tight-lipped patriotism – to austerity, khaki. The Americans arrived and stole the more stunning girls. Uncle Jake was out of the race. Something had snapped in him. He had bluffed his way out of too many poker-hands, put his shirt on too many losers. He began to be a loser himself, and from being a bad example in one decade became inevitably a good one in the next – the model, pathetically thread-bare and unshaven, in a soiled singlet and pants, of what not to be. I came to dread his attempts to engage my ear and explain himself. His rambling account of past triumphs and recent schemes that for one reason or another had gone bung ended always in the same way, a lapse into uneasy silence, then the lame formula: 'If you foller me meanings.' I was growing up. I resented his assumption of an understanding between us and the belief that I was fated somehow to be his interpreter and heir.

'Poor ol' Jake,' my father would sigh, recalling the boy he had grown up with, who had so far outshone him in every sort of daring. He would every now and then slip him a couple of notes, and with his usual shyness of emotion say, 'No mate – it's a loan, I'm keeping tag. You can pay me when your ship comes in.'

My mother had softened by then. She could afford to. So far as she knew I had escaped contagion. 'Poor ol' Jake,' she agreed, and might have felt some regret at her own timidity before the Chances.

So it was Uncle Jake who came to spend his days in the third bedroom of our house, and as he grew more pathetic, as meek as the milk puddings she made because it was the only thing he could keep down, my mother grew fond of him. She nursed him like a baby at the end. It's odd how these things turn out.

A CHANGE OF SCENE

I

Having come like so many others for the ruins, they had been surprised to discover, only three kilometres away, this other survival from the past: a big old-fashioned hotel.

Built in florid neo-baroque, it dated from a period before the Great War when the site was much frequented by Germans, since it had figured, somewhat romanticized, in a passage of Hofmannsthal. The fashion was long past and the place had fallen into disrepair. One corridor of the main building led to double doors that were crudely boarded up, with warnings in four languages that it was dangerous to go on, and the ruined side-wings were given over to goats. Most tourists these days went to the Club Méditerranée on the other side of the bay. But the hotel still maintained a little bathing establishment on the beach (an attendant went down each morning and swept it with a rake) and there was still, on a cliff-top above zig-zag terraces, a pergolated belvedere filled with potted begonias, geraniums and dwarf citrus – an oasis of cool green that the island itself, at this time of year and this late in its history, no longer aspired to. So Alec, who had a professional interest, thought of the ruins as being what kept them here, and for Jason, who was five, it was the beach; but Sylvia, who quite liked ruins and wasn't at all averse to lying half-buried in sand while Jason paddled and Alec, at the entrance to the cabin, tapped away at his typewriter, had settled at first sight for the hotel.

It reminded her, a bit creepily, of pre-war holidays with her parents up on the Baltic – a world that had long ceased to exist except in pockets like this. Half-lost in its high wide corridors, among rococo doors and bevelled gilt-framed mirrors, she almost expected – the past was so vividly present – to meet herself, aged four, in one of the elaborate dresses little girls wore in those days. Wandering on past unreadable numbers, she would come at last to a door that was familiar and would look in and find her grandmother, who was standing with her back to a window, holding in her left hand, so that the afternoon sun broke through it, a jar of homemade cherry syrup, and in her right a spoon. 'Grandma,' she would say, 'the others are all sleeping. I came to you.'

Her grandmother had died peacefully in Warsaw, the year the Germans came. But she was disturbed, re-entering that lost world, to discover how much of it had survived in her buried memory, and how many details came back now with an acid sweetness, like a drop of cherry syrup. For the first time since she was a child she had dreams in a language she hadn't spoken for thirty years – not even with her parents – and was surprised that she could find the words. It surprised her too that Europe – that dark side of her childhood – was so familiar, and so much like home.

She kept that to herself. Alec, she knew, would resent or be hurt by it. She had, after all, spent all but those first years in another place altogether, where her parents were settled and secure as they never could have been in Poland, and it was in that place, not in Europe, that she had grown up, discovered herself and married.

Her parents were once again rich, middle-class people, living in an open-plan house on the North Shore and giving *al fresco* parties at a poolside barbecue. Her father served the well-done steaks with an air of finding this, like so much else in his life, delightful but unexpected. He had not, as a boy in Lvov, had T-bone steaks in mind, nor even a dress factory in Marrickville. These were accidents of fate. He accepted them, but felt he was living the life of an imposter. It added a touch of humorous irony to everything he did. It was her mother who had gone over completely to the New World. She wore her hair tinted a pale mauve, made cheesecake with passion-fruit, and played golf. As for Sylvia, she was simply an odd sort of local. She had had no sense of a foreign past till she came back here and found how European she might be.

Her mother, if she had known the full extent of it, would have found her interest in the hotel 'morbid', meaning Jewish. And it was perverse of her (Alec certainly thought so) to prefer it to the more convenient cabins. The meals were bad, the waiters clumsy and morose, with other jobs in the village or bits of poor land to tend. The plumbing, which looked impressive, all marble and heavy bronze that left a green stain on the porcelain, did not provide water. Alec had no feeling for these ruins of forty years ago. His period was that of the palace, somewhere between eleven and seven hundred BC, when the site had been inhabited by an unknown people, a client state of Egypt, whose language he was working on; a dark, death-obsessed people who had simply disappeared from the pages of recorded history, leaving behind them a few common artefacts, the fragments of a language, and this one city or fortified palace at the edge of the sea.

Standing for the first time on the bare terrace, which was no longer at the edge of the sea, and regarding the maze of open cellars, Alec had been overwhelmed. His eyes, roving over the level stones, were already recording the presence of what was buried here – a whole way of life, richly eventful and shaped by clear beliefs and rituals, that rose grandly for him out of low brick walls and a few precious scratches that were the symbols for corn, salt, water, oil and the names, or attributes, of gods.

What her eyes roamed over, detecting also what was buried, was Alec's face; reconstructing from what passed over features she thought she knew absolutely, in light and in darkness, a language of feeling that he, perhaps, had only just become aware of. She had never, she felt, come so close to what, outside their life together, most deeply touched and defined him. It was work that gave his life its high seriousness and sense of purpose, but he had never managed to make it real for her. When he talked of it he grew excited, but the talk was dull. Now, in the breathlessness of their climb into the hush of sunset, with the narrow plain below utterly flat and parched and the great blaze of the sea beyond, with the child dragging at her arm and the earth under their feet thick with pine-needles the colour of rusty blood, and the shells of insects that had taken their voice elsewhere – in the dense confusion of all this, she felt suddenly that she understood and might be able to share with him now the excitement of it, and had looked up and found the hotel, just the outline of it. Jason's restlessness had delayed for a moment her discovery of what it was.

They had been travelling all day and had come up here when they were already tired, because Alec, in his enthusiasm, could not wait. Jason had grown bored with shifting about from one foot to another and wanted to see how high they were.

'Don't go near the edge,' she told the boy.

He turned away to a row of corn- or oil-jars, big enough each one for a man to crawl into, that were sunk to the rim in stone, but they proved, when he peered in, to be less interesting than he had hoped. No genii, no thieves. Only a coolness, as of air that had got trapped there and had never seeped away.

'It's cold,' he had said, stirring the invisible contents with his arm.

But when Alec began to explain, in words simple enough for the child to understand, what the jars had been used for and how the palace might once have looked, his attention wandered, though he did not interrupt.

Sylvia too had stopped listening. She went back to her own discovery, the big silhouette of what would turn out later to be the hotel.

It was the child's tone of wonder that lingered in her mind: 'It's cold.' She remembered it again when they entered the grand but shabby vestibule of the hotel and she felt the same shock of chill as when, to humour the child, she had leaned down and dipped her arm into a jar.

'What is it?' Jason had asked.

'It's nothing.'

He made a mouth, unconvinced, and had continued to squat there on his heels at the rim.

Alec had grown up on a wheat farm west of Gulgong. Learning early what it is to face bad seasons when a whole crop can fail, or bushfires, or floods, he had developed a native toughness that would, Sylvia saw from his father, last right through into old age. Failure for Alec meant a failure of nerve. This uncompromising view made him hard on occasion, but was the source as well of his golden rightness. Somewhere at the centre of him was a space where honour, fairness, hard work, the belief in a man's responsibility at least for his own fate – and also, it seemed, the possibility of happiness – were given free range; and at the clear centre of all there was a rock, unmoulded as yet, that might one day be an altar. Alec's deficiencies were on the side of strength, and it delighted her that Jason reproduced his father's deep blue eyes and plain sense of having a place in the world. She herself was too rawboned and intense. People called her beautiful. If she was, it was in a way that had too much darkness in it, a mysterious rather than an open beauty. Through Jason she had turned what was leaden in herself to purest gold.

It was an added delight to discover in the child some openness to the flow of things that was also hers, and which allowed them, on occasion, to speak without speaking; as when he had said, up there on the terrace, 'It's cold', at the very moment when a breath from the far-off pile that she didn't yet know was a hotel, had touched her with a premonitory chill.

They were close, she and the child. And in the last months before they came away the child had moved into a similar closeness with her father. They were often to be found, when they went to visit, at the edge of the patio swimming-pool, the old man reading to the boy, translating for him from what Alec called his 'weirdo books', while Jason, in bathing-slip and sneakers, nodded, swung his plump little legs, asked questions, and the old man, with his glasses on the end of his nose and the book resting open a moment on his belly, considered and found analogies.

After thirty years in the garment trade her father had gone back to his former life and become a scholar.

Before the war he had taught philosophy. A radical free-thinker in those days, he had lately, after turning his factory over to a talented nephew, gone right back, past his passion for Wittgenstein and the other idols of his youth, to what the arrogance of that time had made him blind to – the rabbinical texts of his fathers. The dispute, for example, between Rabbi Isserles of Cracow and Rabbi Luria of Ostrov that had decided at Posen, in the presence of the exorcist Joel Baal-Shem, miracle-worker of Zamoshel, that demons have no right over moveable property and may not legally haunt the houses of men.

Her father's room in their ranch-style house at St Ives was crowded with obscure volumes in Hebrew; and even at this distance from the Polish sixteenth century, and the lost communities of his homeland, the questions remained alive in his head and had come alive, in diminutive form, in the boy's. It was odd to see them out there in the hard sunlight of her mother's cactus garden, talking ghosts.

Her mother made faces. Mediaeval nonsense! Alec listened, in a scholarly sort of way, and was engaged at first, but found the whole business in the end both dotty and sinister, especially as it touched the child. He had never understood his father-in-law, and worried sometimes that Sylvia, who was very like him, might have qualities that would emerge in time and elude him. And now Jason! Was the old man serious, or was this just another of his playful jokes?

'No,' Sylvia told him as they drove back in the dark, with Jason sleeping happily on the back seat, 'it's none of the things you think it is. He's getting ready to die, that's all.'

Alec restrained a gesture of impatience. It was just this sort of talk, this light and brutal way of dealing with things it might be better not to mention, that made him wonder at times if he really knew her.

'Well I hope he isn't scaring Jason, that's all.'

'Oh fairy tales, ghost stories – that's not what frightens people.'

'Isn't it?' said Alec. 'Isn't it?'

II

They soon got to know the hotel's routine and the routine of the village, and between the two established their own. After a breakfast of coffee with condensed milk and bread and honey they made their way to the beach: Alec to work, and between shifts at the typewriter to explore the coastline with a snorkel, Sylvia and the child to laze in sand or water.

The breakfast was awful. Alec had tried to make the younger of the two waiters, who served them in the morning, see that the child at least needed fresh milk. For some reason there wasn't any, though they learned from people at the beach that the Cabins got it.

'No,' the younger waiter told them, 'no milk.' Because there were no cows, and the goat's milk was for yogurt.

They had the same conversation every morning, and the waiter, who was otherwise slack, had begun to serve up the tinned milk with a flourish that in Alec's eye suggested insolence. As if to say: *There! You may be Americans* (which they weren't), *and rich* (which they weren't either) *but fresh milk cannot be had. Not on this island.*

The younger waiter, according to the manager, was a Communist. That explained everything. He shook his head and made a clucking sound. But the older waiter, who served them at lunch, a plump, grey-headed man, rather grubby, who was very polite and very nice with the child, was also a Communist, so it explained nothing. The older waiter also assured them there was no milk. He did it regretfully, but the result was the same.

Between them these two waiters did all the work of the hotel. Wandering about in the afternoon in the deserted corridors, when she ought to have been taking a siesta, Sylvia had come upon the younger one having a quiet smoke on a window-sill. He was barefoot, wearing a dirty singlet and rolled trousers. There was a pail of water and a mop beside him. Dirty water was slopped all over the floor. But what most struck her was the unnatural, fishlike whiteness of his flesh – shoulders, arms, neck – as he acknowledged her presence with a nod but without at all returning her smile.

Impossible, she had thought, to guess how old he might be.

Twenty-eight or thirty he looked, but might be younger. There were deep furrows in his cheeks and he had already lost some teeth.

He didn't seem at all disconcerted. She had, he made it clear, wandered into *his* territory. Blowing smoke over his cupped hand (why did they smoke that way?) and dangling his bare feet, he gave her one of those frank, openly sexual looks that cancel all boundaries but the original one; and then, to check a gesture that might have made him vulnerable (it did – she had immediately thought, how boyish!) he glared at her, with the look of a waiter, or peasant, for a foreign tourist. His look had in it all the contempt of a man who knows where he belongs, and whose hands are cracked with labour on his own land, for a woman who has come sightseeing because she belongs nowhere.

Except, she had wanted to protest, it isn't like that at all. It is true I have no real place (and she surprised herself by acknowledging it) but I know what it is to have lost one. That place is gone and all its people are ghosts. I am one of them – a four-year old in a pink dress with ribbons. I am looking for my grandmother. Because all the others are sleeping . . .

She felt differently about the young waiter after that, but it made no odds. He was just as surly to them at breakfast, and just as nasty to the child.

The bay, of which their beach was only an arc, was also used by fishermen, who drew their boats up on a concrete ramp beside the village, but also by the guests from the Cabins and by a colony of hippies who camped in caves at the wilder end.

The hippies were unpopular with the village people. The manager of the hotel told Sylvia that they were dirty and diseased, but they looked healthy enough, and once, in the early afternoon, when most of the tourists had gone in to sleep behind closed shutters, she had seen one of them, a bearded blond youth with a baby on his hip, going up and down the beach collecting litter. They were Germans or Dutch or Scandinavians. They did things with wire, which they sold to the tourists, and traded with the fishermen for octopus or chunks of tuna.

All day the fishermen worked beside their boats on the ramp: mending nets and hanging them from slender poles to dry, or cleaning fish, or dragging octopus up and down on the quayside to remove the slime. They were old men mostly, with hard feet, all the toes stubbed and blackened, and round little eyes. Sometimes, when the child was bored with playing alone in the wet sand, he would wander up the beach and watch them at their work. The quick knives and the grey-blue guts tumbling into the shallows were a puzzle to him, for whom fish were either bright objects that his father showed him when they went out with the snorkel or frozen fingers. The octopus too. He had seen lights on the water at night and his father had explained how the fishermen were using lamps to attract the creatures, who would swarm to the light and could be jerked into the dinghy with a hook. Now he crinkled his nose to see one of the fishermen whip a live octopus out of the bottom of the boat and turning it quickly inside-out, bite into the raw, writhing thing so that its tentacles flopped. He looked at Sylvia and made a mouth. These were the same octopus that, dried in the sun, they would be eating at tomorrow's lunch.

Because the bay opened westward, and the afternoon sun was stunning, their beach routine was limited to the hours before noon.

Quite early, usually just before seven, the young waiter went down and raised the striped canvas awning in front of their beach cabin and raked a few square metres of sand.

Then at nine a sailor came on duty on the little heap of rocks above the beach where a flagpole was set, and all morning he would stand there in his coarse white trousers and boots, with his cap tilted forward and strapped under his chin, watching for sharks. It was always the same boy, a cadet from the Training College round the point. The child had struck up a kind of friendship with him and for nearly an hour sometimes he would 'talk' to the sailor, squatting at his feet while the sailor laughed and did tricks with a bit of cord. Once, when Jason failed to return and couldn't hear her calling, Sylvia had scrambled up the rockface to fetch him, and the sailor, who had been resting on his heel for a bit, had immediately sprung to his feet looking scared.

He was a stocky boy of eighteen or nineteen, sunburned almost to blackness and with very white teeth. She had tried to reassure him that she had no intention of reporting his slackness; but once he had snapped back to attention and then stood easy, he looked right through her. Jason turned on the way down and waved, but the sailor stood very straight against the sky with his trousers flapping and his eyes fixed on the sea, which was milky and thick with sunlight, lifting and lapsing in a smooth unbroken swell, and with no sign of a fin.

After lunch they slept. It was hot outside but cool behind drawn shutters. Then about five-thirty Alec would get up, climb the three kilometres to the palace, and sit alone there on the open terrace to watch the sunset. The facts he was sifting at the typewriter would resolve themselves then as luminous dust; or would spring up alive out of the deepening landscape in the cry of cicadas, whose generations beyond counting might go back here to beginnings. They were dug in under stones, or they clung with shrill tenacity to the bark of pines. It was another language. Immemorial. Indecipherable.

Sylvia did not accompany him on these afternoon excursions, they were Alec's alone. They belonged to some private need. Stretched out in the darkened room she would imagine him up there, sitting in his shirtsleeves in the gathering dusk, the gathering voices, exploring a melancholy he had only just begun to perceive in himself and of which he had still not grasped the depths. He came back, after the long dusty walk, with something about him that was raw and in need of healing. No longer a man of thirty-seven — clever, competent, to whom she had been married now for eleven years — but a stranger at the edge of youth, who had discovered, tremblingly, in a moment of solitude up there, the power of dark.

It was the place. Or now, and here, some aspect of himself that he had just caught sight of. Making love on the high bed, with the curtains beginning to stir against the shutters and the smell of sweat and pine-needles on him, she was drawn into some new dimension of his still mysterious being, and of her own. Something he had felt or touched up there, or which had touched him – his own ghost perhaps, an interior coolness – had brought him closer to her than ever before.

When it was quite dark at last, a deep blue dark, they walked down to one of the quayside restaurants.

There was no traffic on the promenade that ran along beside the water, and between seven and eight-thirty the whole town passed up and down between one headland and the other: family groups, lines of girls with their arms linked, boisterous youths in couples or in loose threes and fours, sailors from the Naval College, the occasional policeman. Quite small children, neatly dressed, played about among rope coils at the water's edge or fell asleep over the scraps of meals. Lights swung in the breeze, casting queer shadows, there were snatches of music. Till nearly one o'clock the little port that was deserted by day quite hummed with activity.

When they came down on the first night, and found the crowds sweeping past under the lights, the child had given a whoop of excitement and cried: 'Manifestazione!' It was, along with gelato, his only word of Italian.

Almost every day while they were in Italy, there had been a demonstration of one sort or another: hospital workers one day, then students, bank clerks, bus-drivers, even highschool kids and their teachers. Always with placards, loud-hailers, red flags and masses of grim-faced police. 'Manifestazione,' Jason had learned to shout the moment they rounded a corner and found even a modest gathering; though it wasn't always true. Sometimes it was just a street market, or an assembly of men in business suits arguing about football or deciding the price of unseen commodities – olives or sheep or wheat. The child was much taken by the flags and the chanting in a language that made no sense. It was all playlike and good-humoured.

But once, overtaken by a fast-moving crowd running through from one street to the next, she had felt herself flicked by the edge of a wave that further back, or just ahead, might have the power to break her grip on the child's hand, or to sweep her off her feet or toss them violently in the air. It was only a passing vision, but she had felt things stir in her that she had long forgotten, and was disproportionately scared.

Here, however, the crowd was just a village population taking a stroll along the quay or gathering at café tables to drink ouzo and nibble side plates of miniature snails; and later, when the breeze came, to watch outdoor movies in the square behind the church.

It was pleasant to sit out by the water, to have the child along, and to watch the crowd stroll back and forth – the same faces night after night. They ate lobster, choosing one of the big, bluish-grey creatures that crawled against the side of a tank, and slices of pink water-melon. If the child fell asleep Alec carried him home on his shoulder, all the way up the steps and along the zig-zag terraces under the moon.

III

One night, the fifth or sixth of their stay, instead of the usual movie there was a puppet-show.

Jason was delighted. They pushed their way in at the side of the crowd and Alec lifted the child on to his shoulders so that he had a good view over the heads of fishermen, sailors from the College and the usual assembly of village youths and girls, who stood about licking icecreams and spitting the shells of pumpkin-seeds.

The little wooden stage was gaudy; blue and gold. In front of it the youngest children squatted in rows, alternately round-eyed and stilled or squealing with delight or terror as a figure in baggy trousers, with a moustache and dagger, strutted up and down on the narrow sill – blustering, bragging, roaring abuse and lunging ineffectually at invisible tormentors, who came at him from every side. The play was both sinister and comic, the moustachioed figure both hero and buffoon. It was all very lively. Big overhead lights threw shadows on the blank wall of the church: pine branches, all needles, and once, swelling abruptly out of nowhere, a giant, as one of the village showoffs swayed aloft. For a moment the children's eyes were diverted by his antics. They cheered and laughed and, leaping up, tried to make their own shadows appear.

The marionette was not to be outdone. Improvising now, he included the insolent spectator in his abuse. The children subsided. There was more laughter and some catcalling, and when the foolish youth rose again he was hauled down, but was replaced, almost at once by another, whose voice drowned the puppet's violent squawking – then by a third. There was a regular commotion.

The little stage-man, maddened beyond endurance, raged up and down waving his dagger and the whole stage shook; over on the wings there was the sound of argument, and a sudden scuffling.

They could see very little of this from where they were pressed in hard against the wall, but the crowd between them and the far-off disturbance began to be mobile. It surged. Suddenly things were out of hand. The children in front, who were being crowded forward around the stage, took panic and began to wail for their parents. There were shouts, screams, the sound of hard blows. In less than a minute the whole square was in confusion and the church wall now was alive with big, ugly shadows that merged in waves of darkness, out of which heads emerged, fists poked up, then more heads. Sylvia found herself separated from Alec by a dozen heaving bodies that appeared to be pulled in different directions and by opposing passions. She called out, but it was like shouting against the sea. Alec and Jason were nowhere to be seen.

Meanwhile the stage, with its gaudy trappings, had been struck away and the little blustering figure was gone. In its place an old man in a singlet appeared, black-haired and toothless, his scrawny body clenched with fury and his mouth a hole. He was screaming without change of breath in the same doll-like voice as the puppet, a high-pitched squawking that he varied at times with grunts and roars. He was inhabited now not only by the puppet's voice but by its tormentors' as well, a pack of violent spirits of opposing factions like the crowd, and was the vehicle first of one, then of another. His thin shoulders wrenched and jerked as if he too was being worked by strings. Sylvia had one clear sight of him before she was picked up and carried, on a great new surging of the crowd, towards the back wall of one of the quayside restaurants, then down what must have been a corridor and on to the quay. In the very last moment before she was free, she saw before her a man covered with blood. Then dizzy from lack of breath, and from the speed with which all this had occurred, she found herself at the water's edge. There was air. There was the safe little bay. And there too were Alec and the boy.

They were badly shaken, but not after all harmed, and in just a few minutes the crowd had dispersed and the quayside was restored to its usual order. A few young men stood about in small groups, arguing or shaking their heads or gesticulating towards the square, but the affair was clearly over. Waiters appeared. They smiled, offering empty tables. People settled and gave orders. They too decided that it might be best, for the child's sake, if they simply behaved as usual. They ordered and ate.

They saw the young sailor who watched for sharks. He and a friend from the village were with a group of girls, and Jason was delighted when the boy recognized them and gave a smart, mock-formal salute. All the girls laughed.

It was then that Sylvia remembered the man she had seen with blood on him. It was the older waiter from the hotel.

'I don't think so,' Alec said firmly. 'You just thought it was because he's someone you know.' He seemed anxious, in his cool, down-to-earth way, not to involve them, even tangentially, in what was a local affair. He frowned and shook his head: *not in front of the boy.*

'No, I'm sure of it,' she insisted. 'Absolutely sure.'

But next morning, at breakfast, there he was quite unharmed, waving them towards their usual table.

'I must have imagined it after all,' Sylvia admitted to herself. And in the clear light of day, with the breakfast tables gleaming white and the eternal sea in the window-frames, the events of the previous night did seem unreal.

There was talk about what had happened among the hotel people and some of the guests from the Cabins, but nothing was clear. It was part of a local feud about fishing rights, or it was political – the puppet-man was a known troublemaker from another village – or the whole thing had no point at all; it was one of those episodes that explode out of nowhere in the electric south, having no cause and therefore requiring no explanation, but gathering up into itself all sorts of hostilities – personal, political, some with their roots in nothing more than youthful high-spirits and the frustrations and closeness of village life at the end of a hot spell. Up on the terraces women were carding wool. Goats nibbled among the rocks, finding rubbery thistles in impossible places. The fishermen's nets, black, brown, umber, were stretched on poles in the sun; and the sea, as if suspended between the same slender uprights, rose smooth, dark, heavy, fading where it imperceptibly touched the sky into mother-of-pearl.

But today the hippies did not appear, and by afternoon the news was abroad that their caves had been raided. In the early hours, before it was light, they had been driven out of town and given a firm warning that they were not to return.

The port that night was quiet. A wind had sprung up, and waves could be heard on the breakwater. The lights swayed overhead, casting uneasy shadows over the rough stones of the promenade and the faces of the few tourists who had chosen to eat. It wasn't cold, but the air was full of sharp little grits and the tablecloths had been damped to keep them from lifting. The locals knew when to come out and when not to. They were right.

The wind fell again overnight. Sylvia, waking briefly, heard it suddenly drop and the silence begin.

The new day was sparklingly clear. There was just breeze enough, a gentle lapping of air, to make the waves gleam silver at the edge of the sand and to set the flag fluttering on its staff, high up on the cliff where the sailor, the same one, was watching for sharks. Jason went to talk to him after paying his usual visit to the fishermen.

Keeping her eye on the child as he made his round of the beach, Sylvia read a little, dozed off, and must for a moment have fallen asleep where Jason had half-buried her in the sand. She was startled into uneasy wakefulness by a hard, clear, cracking sound that she couldn't account for, and was still saying to herself, in the split-second of starting up, *Where am I? Where is Jason?*, when she caught, out of the heel of her eye, the white of his shorts where he was just making his way up the cliff face to his sailor; and in the same instant saw the sailor, above him, sag at the knees, clutching with both hands at the centre of himself, then hang for a long moment in mid-air and fall.

In a flash she was on her feet and stumbling to where the child, crouching on all fours, had come to a halt, and might have been preparing, since he couldn't have seen what had happened, to go on.

It was only afterwards, when she had caught him in her arms and they were huddled together under the ledge, that she recalled how her flight across the beach had been accompanied by a burst of machine-gun fire from the village. Now, from the direction of the Naval College, came an explosion that made the earth shake.

None of this, from the moment of her sitting up in the sand till the return of her senses to the full enormity of the thing, had lasted more than a minute by the clock, and she had difficulty at first in convincing herself that she was fully awake. Somewhere in the depths of herself she kept starting up in that flash of time before the sailor fell, remarking how hot it was, recording the flapping of a sheet of paper in Alec's abandoned typewriter – he must have gone snorkeling or into the village for a drink – and the emptiness of the dazzling sea. *Where am I? Where is Jason?* Then it would begin all over again. It was in going over it the second time, with the child already safe in her arms, that she began to tremble and had to cover her mouth not to cry out.

Suddenly two men dropped into the sand below them. They carried guns. Sylvia and the child, and two or three others who must have been in the water, were driven at gun-point towards the village. There was a lot of gesticulation, and some muttering that under the circumstances seemed hostile, but no actual violence.

They were pushed, silent and unprotesting, into the crowded square. Alec was already there. They moved quickly together, too shocked to do more than touch briefly and stand quietly side by side.

There were nearly a hundred people crushed in among the pine trees, about a third of them tourists. It was unnaturally quiet, save for the abrupt starting up of the cicadas with their deafening beat; then, as at a signal, their abrupt shutting off again. Men with guns were going through the crowd, choosing some and pushing them roughly away towards the quay; leaving others. Those who were left stared immediately ahead, seeing nothing.

One of the first to go was the young waiter from the hotel. As the crowd gave way a little to let him pass, he met Sylvia's eye, and she too looked quickly away; but would not forget his face with the deep vertical lines below the cheekbones and the steady gaze.

There was no trouble. At last about twenty men had been taken and a smaller number of women. The square was full of open spaces. Their group, and the other groups of tourists, looked terribly exposed. Among these dark strangers involved in whatever business they were about — women in coarse black dresses and shawls, men in dungarees — they stood barefoot in briefs and bikinis, showing too much flesh, as in some dream in which they had turned up for an important occasion without their clothes. It was this sense of being both there and not that made the thing for Sylvia so frighteningly unreal. They might have been invisible. She kept waiting to come awake, or waiting for someone else to come awake and release her from a dream that was not her own, which she had wandered into by mistake and in which she must play a watcher's part.

Now one of the gunmen was making an announcement. There was a pause. Then several of those who were left gave a faint cheer.

The foreigners, who had understood nothing of what the gunman said, huddled together in the centre of the square and saw only slowly that the episode was now over; they were free to go. They were of no concern to anyone here. They never had been. They were, in their odd nakedness, as incidental to what had taken place as the pine trees, the little painted ikon in its niche in the church wall, and all those other mute, unseeing objects before whom such scenes are played.

Alec took her arm and they went quickly down the alley to the quay. Groups of armed men were there, standing about in the sun.

Most of them were young, and one, a schoolboy in shorts with a machine-gun in his hand, was being berated by a woman who must have been his mother. She launched a torrent of abuse at him, and then began slapping him about the head while he cringed and protested, hugging his machine-gun but making no attempt to protect himself or move away.

IV

There had been a coup. One of the Germans informed them of it the moment they came into the lobby. He had heard it on his transistor. What they had seen was just the furthest ripple of it, way out at the edge. It had all, it seemed, been bloodless, or nearly so. The hotel manager, bland and smiling as ever, scouring his ear with an elongated finger-nail, assured them there was nothing to worry about. A change of government, what was that? They would find everything – the beach, the village – just the same, only more orderly. It didn't concern them.

But one of the Swedes, who had something to do with the legation, had been advised from the capital to get out as soon as possible, and the news passed quickly to the rest. Later that night a boat would call at a harbour further up the coast. The Club had hired a bus and was taking its foreign guests to meet it, but could not take the hotel people as well.

'What will we do?' Sylvia asked, sitting on the high bed in the early afternoon, with the shutters drawn and the village, as far as one could tell, sleeping quietly below. She was holding herself in.

'We must get that boat,' Alec told her. They kept their voices low so as not to alarm the child. 'There won't be another one till the end of the week.'

She nodded. Alec would talk to the manager about a taxi.

She held on. She dared not think, or close her eyes even for a moment, though she was very tired. If she did it would start all over again. She would see the sailor standing white under the flagpole; then he would cover his belly with his hands and begin to fall. Carefully re-packing their cases, laying out shirts and sweaters on the high bed, she never allowed herself to evaluate the day's events by what she had seen. She clung instead to Alec's view, who had seen nothing; and to the manager's who insisted that except for a change in the administration two hundred miles away things were just as they had always been. The child, understanding that it was serious, played one of his solemn games.

When she caught him looking at her once he turned away and rolled his Dinky car over the worn carpet. 'Hrummm, hrummm,' he went. But quietly. He was being good.

Suddenly there was a burst of gunfire.

She rushed to the window, and pushing the child back thrust her face up close to the slats; but only a corner of the village was visible from here. The view was filled with the sea, which remained utterly calm. When the second burst came, rather longer than the first, she still couldn't tell whether it came from the village or the Naval College or from the hills.

Each time, the rapid clatter was like an iron shutter coming down. It would be so quick.

She turned away to the centre of the room, and almost immediately the door opened and Alec rushed in. He was flushed, and oddly, boyishly exhilarated. He had his typewriter under his arm.

'I'm all right,' he said when he saw her face. 'There's no firing in the village. It's back in the hills. I went to get my stuff.'

There was something in him, some reckless pleasure in his own daring, that scared her. She looked at the blue Olivetti, the folder of notes, and felt for a moment like slapping him, as that woman on the quay had slapped her schoolboy son – she was so angry, so affronted by whatever it was he had been up to out there, which had nothing to do with his typewriter and papers and had put them all at risk.

'Don't be upset,' he told her sheepishly. 'It was nothing. There was no danger.' But his own state of excitement denied it. The danger was in him.

The taxi, an old grey Mercedes, did not arrive till nearly eight. Loaded at last with their luggage it bumped its way into the village.

The scene there was of utter confusion. The bus from the Club, which should have left an hour before, was halted at the side of the road and was being searched. Suitcases were strewn about all over the pavements, some of them open and spilling their contents, others, it seemed, broken or slashed. One of the Club guests had been badly beaten. He was wandering up the middle of the road with blood on his face and a pair of bent spectacles dangling from his ear, plaintively complaining. A woman with grey hair was screaming and being pushed about by two other women and a man – other tourists.

'Oh my God,' Alec said, but Sylvia said nothing. When a boy with a machine-gun appeared they got out quietly and stood at the side of the car, trying not to see what was going on further up the road, as if their situation was entirely different. Their suitcases were opened, their passports examined.

The two gunmen seemed undangerous. One of them laid his hand affectionately on the child's head. Sylvia tried not to scream.

At last they were told to get back into the car, given their passports, smiled at and sent on their way. The pretence of normality was terrifying. They turned away from the village and up the dusty track that Alec had walked each evening to the palace. Thistles poked up in the moonlight, all silver barbs. Dust smoked among sharp stones. Sylvia sank back into the depths of the car and closed her eyes. It was almost over. For the first time in hours she felt her body relax in a sigh.

It was perhaps that same sense of relaxation and relief, an assurance that they had passed the last obstacle, that made Alec reckless again.

'Stop a minute,' he told the driver.

They had come to the top of the ridge. The palace, on its high terrace, lay sixty or seventy metres away across a shallow gully.

'What is it?' Sylvia shouted, springing suddenly awake. The car had turned, gone on a little and stopped.

'No, it's nothing,' he said. 'I just wanted a last look.'

'Alec – ' she began as their headlamps flooded the valley. But before she could say more the lights cut, the driver backed, turned, swung sharply on to the road and they were roaring away at a terrible speed into moonless dark.

The few seconds of sudden illumination had been just enough to leave suspended back there – over the hastily covered bodies, with dust already stripping from them to reveal a cheek, a foot, the line of a rising knee – her long, unuttered cry.

She gasped and took the breath back into her. Jason, half-turned in the seat, was peering out of the back window. She dared not look at Alec.

The car took them fast round bend after bend of the high cliff road, bringing sickening views of the sea tumbling white a hundred feet below in a series of abrupt turns that took all the driver's attention and flung them about so violently in the back of the car that she and Jason had to cling to one another to stay upright. At last, still dizzy with flight, they sank down rapidly to sea level. The driver threw open the door of the car, tumbled out their luggage and was gone before Alec had even produced the money to pay.

'Alec – ' she began.

'No,' he said, 'not now. Later.'

There was no harbour, just a narrow stretch of shingle and a concrete mole. The crowd they found themselves among was packed in so close under the cliff that there was barely room to move. A stiff breeze was blowing and the breakers sent spray over their heads, each wave, as it broke on the concrete slipway, accompanied by a great cry from the crowd, a salty breath. They were drenched, cold, miserable. More taxis arrived. Then the bus. At last, after what seemed hours, a light appeared far out in the blackness and the ship came in, so high out of the water that it bounced on the raging surface like a cork.

'We're almost there,' Alec said, 'we're almost there,' repeating the phrase from time to time as if there were some sort of magic in it.

The ship stood so high out of the water that they had to go in through a tunnel in the stern that was meant for motor vehicles. They jammed into the cavernous darkness, driven from behind by the pressure of a hundred bodies with their individual weight of panic, pushed in hard against suitcases, wooden crates, hastily tied brown parcels, wire baskets filled with demented animals that squealed and stank. Coming suddenly from the cold outside into the closed space, whose sides resounded with the din of voices and strange animal cries, was like going deep into a nightmare from which Sylvia felt she would never drag herself alive. The huge chamber steamed. She couldn't breathe. And all through it she was in terror of losing her grip on the child's hand, while in another part of her mind she kept telling herself: I should release him. I should let him go. Why drag *him* into this?

At last it was over. They were huddled together in a narrow place on the open deck, packed in among others; still cold, and wetter than ever now as the ship plunged and shuddered and the fine spray flew over them, but safely away. The island sank in the weltering dark.

'I don't think he saw, do you?' Alec whispered. He glanced at her briefly, then away. 'I mean, it was all so quick.'

He didn't really want her to reply. He was stroking the boy's soft hair where he lay curled against her. The child was sleeping. He cupped the blond head with his hand, and asked her to confirm that darkness stopped there at the back of it, where flesh puckered between bony knuckles, and that the child was unharmed. It was himself he was protecting. She saw that. And when she did not deny his view, he leaned forward across the child's body and pressed his lips, very gently, to her cheek.

Their heads made the apex of an unsteady triangle where they leaned together, all three, and slept. Huddled in among neighbours, strangers with their troubled dreams, they slept, while the ship rolled on into the dark.

IN TRUST

There is to begin with the paraphernalia of daily living: all those objects, knives, combs, coins, cups, razors, that are too familiar, too worn and stained with use, a door-knob, a baby's rattle, or too swiftly in passage from hand to mouth or hand to hand to arouse more than casual interest. They are disposable, and are mostly disposed of without thought. Tram tickets, matchboxes, wooden serviette rings with a poker design of poinsettias, buttonhooks, beermats, longlife torch batteries, the lids of Doulton soup tureens, are carted off at last to a tip and become rubble, the sub-stratum of cities, or are pulped and go to earth; unless, by some quirk of circumstance, one or two examples are stranded so far up the beach in a distant decade that they become collectors' items, and then so rare and evocative as to be the only survivors of their age.

So it is in the life of objects. They pass out of the hands of their first owners into a tortoiseshell cabinet, and then, whole or in fragments it scarcely matters, on to the shelves of museums. Isolated there, in the oddness of their being no longer common or repeatable, detached from their history and from the grime of use, they enter a new dimension. A quality of uniqueness develops in them and they glow with it as with the breath of a purer world – meaning only that we see them clearly now in the light of this one. An oil-lamp, a fragment of cloth so fragile that we feel the very grains and precious dust of its texture (the threads barely holding in their warp and woof), a perfume flask, a set of taws, a strigil, come wobbling towards us, the only angels perhaps we shall ever meet, though they bear no message but their own presence: *we are here*.

It is in a changed aspect of time that we recognize them, as if the substance of it – a denseness that prevented us from looking forward or too far back – had cleared at last. We see these objects and ourselves as co-existent, in the very moment of their first stepping out into their own being and in every instant now of their long pilgrimage towards us, in which they have gathered the fingerprints of their most casual users and the ghostly but still powerful presence of the lives they served.

None of our kind come to us down that long corridor. Only the things they made and made use of, which still somehow keep contact with them. We look through the cracked bowl to the lips of children. Our hand on an axe-handle fits into an ancient groove and we feel the jarring of tree-trunk on bone. Narrowly avoiding through all their days the accidents that might have toppled them from a shelf, the flames, the temper tantrums, the odd carelessness of a user's hand, they are still with us. We stare and are amazed. Were they once, we ask ourselves, as undistinguished as the buttons on our jacket or a stick of roll-on deodorant? Our own utensils and artefacts take on significance for a moment in the light of the future. Small coins glow in our pockets. Our world too seems vividly, unbearably present, yet mysteriously far off.

Each decade a new class of objects comes into being as living itself creates new categories of use. After the centuries of the Bowl (plain or decorated with rice-grains, or with figures, some of them gods, in hieratic poses, or dancing or making love) come the centuries of the Wheel, the age of Moving-across-the-Surface-of-the-Earth, from the ox-cart to the Silver Spur.

Later again, it is not only objects that survive and can be collected. Images too, the shadowy projection of objects, live on to haunt us with the immediacy of what was: figures alone or in groups, seated with a pug dog on their knees or stiffly upright in boating costume beside an oar; a pyramid of young men in flannel slacks and singlets holding the difficult pose forever, blood swelling their necks as they strain upward, set on physical perfection; three axemen beside a fence, leaning their rough heads together; the crowd round an air-balloon. Bearded, monocled, or in hoop skirts under parasols, and with all their flesh about them, they stare boldly out of a century of Smiles . . .

Not long ago, in the Museum of the Holocaust at Jerusalem, a middle-aged American, an insurance assessor, gave a sudden cry before one of the exhibits, threw out his arms, and while two maiden ladies from Hannibal, Missouri, looked on in helpless dismay, fell slowly to his knees – then, clutching his chest, even more slowly to the pavement at their feet. They tried to help him, but he did not get up again.

His tour companions had found him difficult, a loud, dull fellow. He had informed them that he made eighty-five thousand dollars a year, had a house at Fresno and a ranch near Santa Fe, was divorced from a woman called Emmeline who had cost him his balls in alimony, had a son who was on heroin, voted for Reagan, hated the Ruskies and that goddamned Ayatollah – the usual stuff. He wore a gold ring on one finger with a Hebrew letter (he was Jewish) and now, right in the middle of a nine-day tour of all the holy places, Christian, Jewish and you-name-it, he was dead. He had, it seems, been confronted here with the only surviving record of his family, a group picture taken forty years before on the welcoming-ramp at Treblinka: his mother, father, two sisters, his six-year-old self, all with the white breath pouring out of their mouths in the January cold, heads turned in half-profile and slightly lifted towards the darkness just ahead, with beyond it (though this they could not have foreseen) a metre of roughened museum wall and the door into another country.

It was that vision of himself in the same dimension as the long dead that struck the man and struck him down: that rather than any recollection of the moment when the shot was taken. To see thus, from the safe distance of an American travel-group he had joined in Athens, Greece, that lost gathering to which he most truly belonged, and to see at last just where it was (despite the forty years detour) that he was headed, had pushed him to the only step he could have taken – straight through the wall; and an error made nearly half a century ago, when an officer had breathed too lightly on a rubber stamp, was righted at last and a number restored to sequence. His cry was a home-coming.

His fellow-travellers on this later occasion, though shaken, went on to the rest of the experience: images, objects, carefully worked facts and descriptions. Only that one man went right to the centre, stepping through a wall that was in the end as insubstantial as breath, and on into flame.

Gillian Vaughan came back from her great-aunt Connie's with a present, a large and rather dog-eared envelope that she was clutching with fervour to her schoolgirl breast and which she refused at first to show.

Her mother was disconcerted, and not for the first time, by the child's intractable oddity. At just eleven Gillian was old-fashioned – that was the kind way of putting it, and stubbornly so; it was something she would not outgrow. It worried the mother, since her own nature was uncomplicated, easy (or so she thought) and she would have wished for the same qualities in her child. 'Gillian darling,' she protested now, but mildly, she was easily hurt, 'what on earth? – I mean, what are we to *do* with them?'

'Nothing,' the girl replied. 'Look after them, that's all. I said I would and I will. You don't have to worry. I'll do it. They're Aunt Connie's most treasured possessions.'

The envelope contained five x-ray photographs, and the curious child had chosen them.

Connie Hermiston, Great-aunt Connie, was eighty-seven. For the past year or more she had been passing on to her various nieces, and to those grand-nieces with whom she had contact, the family relics she was responsible for and which she wanted to leave now in younger hands.

She was not herself a collector, but she had, because of her extreme age, become the custodian over the years of other peoples' treasures – though treasures was too large a word for the jumble of bits and pieces she had stacked for safe-keeping in cupboards, drawers and odd cartons and hat-boxes beside her wardrobe. Other peoples' sentiments or passions might be more accurate, as they attached themselves, mysteriously sometimes, to a kewpie doll on a black crook, from the Brisbane Exhibition of 1933, a fan made of peacock-feathers, several evening bags, pearl-handled cake-forks, a little lounge-suite made of iridescent china, medals, pushers-and-spoons, Coronation cups, christening dresses, handpainted birthday cards with celluloid lace edges. None of it had any real value, it was just family stuff; but each item had its pedigree, with the name attached (so far as Great-aunt Connie's memory could be trusted) of a Hermiston or a Cope or a Vaughan or a Glynn-Jones. Offered something out of this treasure house that should be hers, some piece of family history that she should be the one to carry forward, Gillian had chosen the x-rays. Only now, when she regarded them with her mother's eyes, did she see that her choice might be peculiar. She sighed, unhappy to discover that she had put herself, yet again, on the *odd* side of things.

'His name was Green,' she said solemnly, as if the specific detail might make a difference. 'John Winston Green.' She meant the subject of the x-rays, which showed, in various degrees of ghostliness, in left and right profile but also frontally, the thorax and jaw of a young man.

Her mother's sister, Aunt Jude, who had been at the window, came up now, and leaning down she kissed the child on the top of the head, at the parting where her hair was drawn in pigtails.

Gillian looked up at her. Jude Hermiston smiled. She took the dusty package from her sister and examined it. 'Let's look,' she said, 'shall we?'

She slipped the first x-ray out of the package, then one by one the rest.

She had seen them before. Years back, on visits to Aunt Connie's, she too had been allowed to take from their envelope the stiff, transparent sheets, and holding them to the light had seen him, this bit of him: John Winston Green, Aunt Connie's young man. Odd emotions stirred in her. They seemed her own, but were too deeply overlaid with what she had heard and caught breath of from Aunt Connie for her to be sure. Except that the emotions were powerful and real – a kind of astonished awe as before a common mystery.

The profile, its lovely line: where the base of the skull, so round you could feel it in the cup of your hand, swooped down to the neck, with the vertebrae, all ghostly grey, stacked delicately one above the other, almost pearly, and the Adam's apple a transparent bump. The left profile; then, minimally but perceptibly different, the right.

The Adam's apple: how touchingly present and youthful it was. You felt it in your own throat like a lump of apple, or like a difficult word. And the firm line upwards to the jaw. In the third and fourth image the head was turned sharply right – John Winston Green might have been giving the eyes-right salute to an unseen general; but the thorax appeared straight on and all the elements were changed; you saw the contained energy in the throat muscles, the strain of the tendons of the neck. The power and will of a whole being was there. You felt the squareness, the solidity of it all the way down to the footsoles, the stern discipline, held breath in the ribcage, the pushing upward of the skull, the way gravity tugged, created weight (say eleven stone six) and held it to earth.

The neck seemed thick in the front views. The vertebrae in their pile like children's bricks were too squarely packed. But in profile you caught the delicacy of the thing, and it was this that touched and moved Jude now as it had moved her twenty years ago. The young man's adam's apple rose in her throat. A word it was, that he had intended to speak but could not, because he had to hold his breath for the machine; a thought that had sparked in the skull, travelled at lightning speed down that luminous cord and got stuck in his throat. It was there, still visible.

John Winston Green, Aunt Connie's young man, had worked as a clerk in the Bank of Queensland. He was an oarsman as well, wrote poetry, and had died at Bullecourt in France, in 1917. The x-rays were Aunt Connie's last memento of him. All the rest, letters with poems in them, snapshots of occasions she still remembered and could describe – picnics at Peel Island, tennis parties, regattas – and all the small gifts he had sent her when he was away on rowing trips in the south, and from Paris and Egypt, had been consumed in a fire nearly thirty years ago. Since they hadn't at first been worth keeping, the x-rays had been stored in a garage and had alone survived. 'They were the only thing he gave me that lasted,' Aunt Connie could say in her dry, no-nonsense manner. 'Isn't it odd? The most faithful representations of all they were – in the end. Why shouldn't I love them best of all?' This, Jude guessed, is what she must have told her grand-niece Gillian. It is what she had told Jude.

There are natural lines of descent in a family. They are not always the direct ones. It is proper that the objects people care for should find their way down through them, from hand to hand and from heart to heart. 'She is my true mother,' Jude Hermiston had told herself once, 'and this young man, of whom I have only this brief, illuminating glimpse, is my true father. That lump in his throat must be my name.'

She restored the last of the x-rays to their package. She smiled, and so did the child. And Harriet Vaughan, who was fond of her sister, watched her daughter take the package and clasp it once again, so solemnly, to her breast.

'What was the choice, darling?' she asked, though of course it could not matter.

'Oh spoons,' the child told her lightly, 'that belonged to grandma. Moya Cope got them. And a little case for jewels.'

Harriet looked again at the ancient envelope the child had hold of and was resigned: not to the entrance of these odd relics among them, but to her daughter, this child who had come to her, she thought, like a stranger, having no likeness she could discover either to Eric or to herself, an utterly dear and separate being whose very difficulty she loved.

'You don't mind, mummy, do you? I mean – I know the spoons were more *valuable*.'

'Of course I don't,' her mother told her, and leaned down to kiss the child. 'You funny bunny! Of course I don't.'

A TRAVELLER'S TALE

I

There is a point in the northern part of the state, or rather, a line that runs waveringly across it, where the vegetation changes within minutes. A cataclysmic second a million or more years back has pushed two land masses violently together, the one open savannah country with rocky outcrops and forests of blue-grey feathery gums, the other sub-tropical scrub. You arrive at the crest of a ridge and a whole new landscape swings into view. Hoop pines and bunya command the skyline. There are palm-trees, banana plantations. Leisurely broad rivers that seem always in flood go rolling seaward between stands of plumed and scented cane. It is as if you had dozed off at the wheel a moment and woken a whole day further on.

Poor white country. Little makeshift settlements, their tin roofs extinguished with paint or still rawly flashing, huddle round a weatherboard spire. Spindly windmills stir the air. There are water-tanks in the yards, half-smothered under bougainvillea; sheds painted a rusty blood-colour, all their timbers awry but the old nails strongly holding, slide sideways at an alarming angle; and everywhere, scattered about on burnt-off slopes and in naked paddocks, the parts of Holdens, Chevvies, Vanguards, Pontiacs, and the engines of heavy transports, spring up like bits of industrial sculpture or the remains of highway accidents awaiting a poor man's resurrection. A tin lizzie only recently taken off the road suddenly explodes and takes wing as half a dozen chooks come squarking and flapping from the sprung interior.

Nothing is ever finished here, but nothing is done with either. Everything is in process of being dismantled, reconstructed, recycled, and turned by the spirit of improvisation into something else. A place of transformations.

At one point on the highway, surprisingly balanced above ground and about the same length as the Siamese Royal Barge, is the Big Banana, a representation of that fruit in garish yellow plaster. Two hundred miles further on and you come to the Big Pineapple, also in plaster, and with a gallery under the crown for viewing the surrounding hills. Between the two you are in another country. Men work in shorts in the fields and are of one colour with the earth, a fiery brick-red. Kids go barefoot, moving off the track on to the tufted bank with a studied slowness, as if they had heard somewhere that there is a fortune to be made by getting struck. Little girls in faded frocks hang over gates, dispiritedly waving, or in bare yards sit dangling their legs from an elongated inner-tube that has been hoisted aloft and found new life as a swing.

Every significant happening here belongs to the past and was of a geological nature. A line of extinct volcanoes whose fires were dashed out several millennia back, leaving a heap of dark, cone-shaped clinkers, are the most striking components of the scene. Cooling as they have in odd shapes, they have ceased to be terrible and are merely curious. Even their names in the Aboriginal language, which were often crude but did at least speak up for the mysteries, have dwindled on the local tongue to mere unpronounceables, old body-jokes whose point, if there was one, has been lost in the commonness of use.

It is one of my duties as an emissary of the Arts to bring news of our national culture to this slow back-water. My name is Adrian Trisk, livewire and leprechaun; or more properly, Projects Officer with the Council for the Arts.

The routine is always the same. Advertisements are placed in the 'Canefarmers' Gazette' or the 'Parish Recorder' and the Shire Hall hired for say Tuesday night at seven thirty, with supper provided and no charge. I show slides of contemporary Australian painting and sometimes a film, using the projector that is housed, along with the paraphernalia for Sunday Mass, in a hutch at the back of the hall; or I lecture on the life and works of an Australian poet. Nothing rigorous. Usually there are no more than a dozen in the audience; sometimes, in bad weather or when my appearance coincides with a meeting of the Country Women's Association, just two or three. Most difficult of all are places like Karingai where the population is 'mixed' – that is, part Australian, part Italian, part Aboriginal, part Indian; and worst of all is Karingai itself, where even the Indian population is split into sects that worship at rival temples. I make certain, so far as these things can be arranged, that towns like Karingai appear on my itinerary no more than once every two or three years. Bridging the gap is all very well, but there is a limit to what a man can do with the discovery poems of Douglas Stewart and a slide evening with William Dobell.

The culture business, it's a box of knives! I could show wounds. I have been at it now for half a lifetime: twenty years as an expatriate with the British Council in Sarawak, Georgetown, Abadan; a stint at a West African University; two years as tutor to the brother-in-law of a sheikh – I'm not altogether without experience. But at fifty-six I have no firm foot on the ladder. There are always the young, pouring out of the universities with their heads full of schemes for converting the masses; little blond geniuses, all charm and killer-instinct, looking for cover while they finish a novel; girls with a flair for doling out rejection-slips and serving coffee to visiting celebrities; streamlined lesbians who know *just* how to re-organize everything so that it *works*. I have enemies everywhere, and they have not scrupled to poison the ear of authority with insinuations that I am not what I claim to be: that my post at that flyblown university, for example, was not on the teaching side but in catering. Life is a constant struggle.

I meet it with energy. Boundless energy. Nothing disarms people so completely, I have discovered, as breathless enthusiasm. Hopping about on one foot, crowing, chuckling, slapping one's thigh, pinching people's elbows in an excess of delight at finding them alive, well and just where they might be expected to be; peppering the speech with absurd formulations like '*Aren't* we all having a marvel-

lous time? *Isn't* this just what the doctor ordered?', or such patent
insincerities as 'Hello there, all you lovely, *lovely* people!'; above
all buttering the ear with flattery, flattery so excessive that only the
most hardened egotist could take it seriously and lesser men curl up
with embarrassment – these are powerful weapons in the right
hand, and immediately establish the user as a harmless crank, too
clownlike, too scatty, too effusive and highly strung to be a master
of calculation.

Well, it's one of the strategies. In fact I am full of good will and
want only to be left alone to make my way and to enjoy a moment
of late sunshine at the top of the tree, but to achieve that I must
protect myself, and protecting myself means playing the buffoon
and avoiding places like Karingai where for reasons quite beyond
my control (like the fact that the wretched Indians have rival
temples) I will be left presenting my Brett Whiteley extravaganza to
the wife of the Methodist minister, a retired timbergetter who is
rewriting the works of Henry Lawson and the hapless two-year
incumbent of the one-teacher school.

II

I had finished my lecture and was waiting for the minister's wife,
C. of E. on this occasion, to lead me to supper. The coffee-urn and
the trestle table laden with sausage-rolls, anzacs, rainbow cake,
date-loaf and pavlova were waiting at the end of the hall, presided
over by two large-bosomed ladies who had spent the whole of my
talk in setting it up, its impressive abundance determined less by the
expected size of the audience than by their own sense of what was
due to the Arts – the Arts, out here, meaning Cookery, of which
the higher forms are cake-decoration and the ornamental bottling
of carrots. The platform lights had been removed, the extension
lead and projector, like some image of local veneration, had been
restored to its hutch.

'If y' don't mind, Mr Trist, I'd appreciate a few words. You might
'ear somethin' t' yer advantage.'

It was the legal phrase that startled me – I was used to the little
confusion about my name.

The speaker was a diminutive woman of sixty-five or seventy, very battered looking, whom I had taken when she first came in, she was so dark-eyed and brown, for one of the Indians; except that she wore a hat, a crumpled straw with two roses pinned to the brim, and a pair of white gloves that suggested Anglo-Saxon formality, the effort a woman makes who has to see her lawyer about the terms of a separation, or a doctor for what might prove, if luck is against her, to be a fatal illness – occasions she would want, later, to remember and be dressed for.

She had made no pretence, I noticed, of following my lecture, though it is one of my finest and had been delivered with all my customary verve. 'Arthur Boyd and the Mystic Bride' was not, it seems, her cup of tea. Easing off her shoes with a series of gasps and sighs that was itself very nearly mystical, and which she in no way attempted to hide, she had slumped deeper and deeper into the canvas chair, blinking her eyes at one moment, as if what she saw on a vivid slide alarmed her, then once more sinking from view; and had difficulty, when it was over, in getting back into her shoes. An inconsiderate woman, who astonished me now by announcing: 'It's t' do with that article you writ on Alicia Vale.'

Now there is such a paper. It is one of several on a wide range of topics – West Nigerian gold-weights, Renaissance scissors, house interiors in Muscat and Oman. My publications at least are indisputable and can be produced as proof positive of their own existence. It's a little *coup* it gives me great satisfaction to produce. But that my Vale monograph, which isn't entirely unknown to followers of the Diva, should have found its way to Karingai! And into the hands of this odd, ungrammatical woman!

'You've read it?' I said foolishly.

She ignored the question. 'I can't talk 'ere, it isn't the right place. But I reckon you'll be interested in some information I got.' She worked her mouth a little, having lost control for the moment of her teeth, which she must also have assumed for the occasion. She snapped, got them fixed again, and went on. 'And *things*. I got some'v 'er things. 'Ere's me address. I've writ it on this bitta paper. I'll expecher round ten.'

She thrust a page of ruled note-paper into my hand, said 'Thanks' – once to me and again to the minister's wife – and was off.

'Who was *that*?' I asked, and stood staring at the floral back.

Mrs Logan allowed her lips to form a superior smile. 'Oh that, poor soul, was our Mrs Judge. She's quite a character. Lives out near the Indians.'

My first thought, I should admit, was that it was a trap. My passion for the Diva, my obsession we might as well call it, with her life, her records, her relics, is pretty well-known at the Council and I have enemies who would be happy to see me discomforted.

As a matter of simple caution I pushed the scrap of paper into my breast pocket as if it were of no importance, rubbed my hands together in a gesture of exaggerated delight at the prospect of sausage rolls and pavlova (over-doing it as usual to the point where it declared itself to be quite plainly an act) and waited for Mrs Logan to move. She did not. She was observing me with amused but dangerous detachment.

She was a tall young woman whose husband had hopes of being a bishop. She was bearing their period in the wilderness with a good grace but was impatient. It showed. Her words snapped, her fingers flew at things, the tendons in her neck were strained. Her intelligence, finding no object out here, had begun to spin away from her, and since she leaned so much towards it, had set her off balance. She was poised but unstill, and seemed quite capable, I thought, of taking an interest in me, and in the unfortunate Mrs Judge, out of boredom, or because no larger opportunity offered itself for revealing how superior she was to the follies and passions of men.

'You mean to go?' she asked.

I tried to laugh it off.

'Oh well, it depends, doesn't it? On how the morrow feels. I mean, you never know, do you? Perhaps it will be a Mrs Judge day.'

She seemed to find this very comical. I did a little jig as if I too recognized the absurdity of the thing; and experienced a wave of nausea at my own impiety. The bishop's wife, no doubt, had other notions of what was holy.

But I had saved myself, that's what mattered, and looked on the three sausage rolls I forced down, and the two slices of pavlova, as a proper expiation, and a proper snub to my hostess, who had assumed that in the matter of pavlovas at least there would be a certain complicity between us. In fact I loathe pavlova; but this is a question of taste, not Taste, and I took two slices very willingly to make amends. It was only when I got outside at last, and felt the dense sub-tropical night about me, the restless palm-leaves fretting and rising, the low stars, the beating of wings and bell-notes in distended throats, the heavy scent of decay that is also the sweet smell of change – it was only then that I let myself off the leash and felt my heart quicken with a sense that even the dreaded Karingai might be the site of a turn in my fortunes, some unique and unlooked-for revelation. A magic name had been spoken and Mrs Judge's address was burning above my breast.

But of course I would go!

III

I found the house easily enough. One of five unpainted weather-boards on high stumps, it stood apart from the rest of the town on a narrow ridge. The other houses belonged to Indians. Plump dark children, the youngest of them naked, splashed about in mud-puddles in the front yards; chickens rushed out squawking; a lean dog tied to a fence-post stood on its four legs and yowled. Morning-glory, running wild in every direction, hauled fences down till they were almost horizontal, swathed the trunks of palms, was piled feet deep above water-tanks and out-house roofs. The big purple blossoms were starred with moisture. From beneath came the faint hum of insects and the smell almost overpoweringly sweet, of rotting vegetation.

Climbing the wooden steps, which had long since lost their rails, I paused at the lattice door and prepared to knock.

The woman was there immediately. She must have been waiting in the shadows beyond. Darker than I remembered, she had, in the clear light of day, a driven look, as if she had been hungry for twenty and maybe thirty years for something that had hollowed her out from within and which the black eyes had slowly sunk towards.

She wore the same blue floral, but it was beltless now, and her feet on the dry verandah boards were misshapen and bare.

'Come on in,' she said, peering over my shoulder to make sure there was no one with me; then stood and smiled. 'I reckoned you wouldn' let me down.' She turned into the hallway with its worn linoleum. 'Come on out t' the kitchen an' I'll make a cuppa.'

Indicating a chair at the scrubbed-wood table, she used her forearm to push back mess – jam-tins, scraps of half-eaten toast, several dirty mugs; then filled a kettle, scooped tea from a tin with Japanese ladies in kimonos on each of its faces, and sat. Behind her, on the wood stove, the kettle began to hiss.

'As I was sayin',' she began, as if our conversation of the previous evening had never been interrupted, 'I got information t' give, seein' as yer interested in 'er.'

'Alicia Vale?'

She laughed. 'Well I don't mean the Queen a' Sheba.'

She glanced round the smoke-grimed kitchen, cleared a further space between us, as if she were preparing an area amid the chaos where large facts could be established, and with a new light in her eyes, thrust her hand out and opened her fist.

Coiled in her palm was an enamel bracelet of exquisite red and gold, in the form of a serpent. Beside it, two tiny Fabergé eggs.

She was delighted with my look of astonishment and gave a harsh, high-pitched laugh.

'There! You didn't expect that, didja? I thought that'd surprise you.' She set the three pieces down and turned away to haul the kettle off the stove. 'You oughta know that piece if you're an expert. She wore that in *Lakmé*. New York, nineteen o-five.'

It looked even more extraordinary among the breakfast litter of the table than it might have done in the museum where it belonged: one of those elaborate pieces that were created for her first by Lalique and later by Tiffany – lilies, serpents, salamanders, birds of paradise, all in the blue-green or red-gold of the period and intended to be worn off-stage or on, tributes to the fact that her own plumed splendour was continuous with that of the creatures she played, and that these ornaments of her fantasy-life in Babylon or India belonged equally to the world she moved in at Deauville and Monte Carlo, at Karlsbad, Baden Baden, Capri. The thing writhed. It flashed its tail and threw off sparks. It was solid metal and had survived. I turned it and read the signature.

'Oh, it's genuine alright,' she told me, pouring tea. She gave a wry chuckle. 'I took one look at you and I reckoned you'd be the one. I knew it right off. This one, I told meself — he'll believe, if on'y the bracelet. And he does! Here, young feller, drink yer tea.'

She sipped noisily and watched me over the rim of her cup.

'Y'see,' she said, suddenly serious, 'I trustcher. I gotta trust someone and you're it. I've decided t' come out a'hiding.'

She let this sink in.

'I s'pose you know she was back 'ere in o-six.'

'O-eight,' I corrected, glad at last to prove, after so many surprises, my expertise. 'There was a tour in o-three and another in o-eight — *Lucrezia, Lucia, Semiramide, Adriana Lecouvreur.*' I had it all off pat.

'Yair,' she said. 'Well she was 'ere in o-six as well, that's what I'm tellin' yer. O-six.'

I was in no position to argue. Nobody in fact knows where Vale was in nineteen hundred and six; the whole year is a blank. In o-five she was in San Francisco, New York, Brussels, London, Paris and St Petersburg. In o-seven in South Africa, Vienna, Budapest, Warsaw, Berlin, and was back in London again to close the season. But in o-six nothing. The theory is that she had a minor breakdown and was hiding out in the south of France. More romantic commentators suggest a trip to China in the company of a Crown Prince, or a time in Persia with an Armenian munitions manufacturer who later, it is true, bought her a house in Hampstead and her first motor. But no one, so far as I know, has mentioned Australia.

'She spent the time,' the woman informed me without emphasis, though her little black eyes were as lively as jumping beans — she was enjoying her moment of triumph — 'in a suite in the Hotel Australia in Melbourne. And that's where us twins were born, me and a brother. I am Alicia Vale's daughter!'

She opened up like a fist and presented herself, as she had

previously presented the bracelet; all without warning, a glittering jewel. As if to say: 'There! If you believed in that you should believe in me. We're all of a piece.'

She sat back sucking her gums and grinning, delighted at having played her little scene with so much skill, and at having, for a second time, so convincingly set me back.

'You can put that down now,' she told me, indicating the bracelet. 'We're talking about me.'

I have spent nearly twenty years following the career of that extra-ordinary woman, through newspaper articles, reviews, programmes, opera house account-books (my little paper is a run-up to what I hope may be a full biography), and had, even before I made my first venture upon the documentary records, been spellbound for another twenty by the legend of her and by the thin, pure voice (unhappily a mere ghost of itself) that comes to us from the primitive recording-machines of the period.

She was still singing after the war – after 1918, that is – but only simple things: a Schubert lullaby, 'Home Sweet Home'. Such is the magic of her art that even these become, in her rendering of them, occasions of the most poignant beauty; as if the simple melody of 'Home Sweet Home' were being plucked out of the air by an angel banished forever from the forests of Ceylon or the Gardens of Babylon, bringing with it, out of that lost world, only a radiant and disembodied breath. As an adolescent I would listen to those recordings with locked eyes; imagining from photographs the exotic realm out of which it was climbing, in which a common farmgirl from the South Coast had been transformed by her own genius, and elaborate machines for making ground-fog, clouds and columns that can dissolve before the eyes on a view of endless horizons, into a creature of mythical power and beauty, a princess with the gift of immortality or abrupt extinction in her, a bird of paradise, an avenging angel – though she might also on occasion, and without one's sensing the least disjunction, appear in the pages of an inter-national scandal-sheet, where her notorious language and ordinary, not to say vulgar affairs, like the exploits of the gods in their earthly passages, were transfigured and redeemed by the glory that came trailing after.

A coruscating meteor. Given that a meteor, all light and sparkle as it pours across the heavens, is at centre stone. Nothing so convinces us of her ethereal majesty as the fact that she was also a hard-headed business-woman, who swore like a navvy (and got away with it), drank three bottles of Guinness at breakfast, and was surrounded wherever she went by a motley circus of book-makers, card-sharps, stand-over men and a whole chorus-line of pale young fellows with shoulders, who made her every entrance a spectacle. On stage she was, as often as not, a queen disguised as a gipsy. Off-stage she was the gipsy itself, demanding that she be treated as a queen.

In her later years, when she lived on the harbour at Kirribilli, she became a kind of native Gorgon. I have a photograph, taken at her seventieth birthday-celebration at Anthony Hordern's, where she is caught, very grand and baleful, among a group of admirers – all elderly, all male, and all looking strangely fossilized, as if she had just that moment turned her hooded eyes upon them. Yet the occasion itself is as innocent as a children's party. The little cakes in their silver dishes are made up to look like snails, frogs, piglets; there are jelly-moulds, and a huge, heart-shaped cake with a knife in it and a ring of hard-flamed miniature candles.

She had survived and would live to eighty. Not for her the tragic destiny of Phar Lap or Les Darcy, done to death, their proud hearts broken, by foreigners. They're a tougher breed than the men, these colonial girls: the Alicias, the Melbas, the Marjories, the Joans. They conquer the world and come home to die in the suburbs, in their own swan's-down beds . . . But to be told now, after nearly half a century, that the catalogue is incomplete; that to the collection of Riccio grotesques and Kaendler Meissen, the gold Rolls-Royce, the Louis Seize commodes by Dubois and Riesener, the Daum vases, the Tiffany lamps and jewels, the costumes in which she filled out with her own marvellous presence courtesans, princesses, village girls afflicted with somnambulism, we must add an unacknowledged child – real, human – and especially, after so long *this* child, 'our

Mrs Judge', a weatherbeaten, slatternly but oddly impressive woman at a grubby kitchen table in Karingai, who has appeared at last to claim her place in the glittering tale and to demand, with an authority that might be a shadow of the Diva's own, that I should stand up now and be the first to acknowledge her! Is this how the great tests present themselves to us? At ten-thirty in the morning, in a country kitchen, in a place like Karingai?

The woman set herself before me. She dared me to believe and take up her cause.

I was spared at the last moment by a footstep on the verandah. A man appeared, a big man in wellingtons. He had the soft-footed, respectful air of a visitor, but one who knew the place and was at home. The woman turned to face him. She made no attempt to hide the bracelet, or the fact that there existed between us a state of high drama.

'This,' she said, and might have been speaking to herself, 'is my husband George.' She got up, turned away to the dresser and brought another cup.

The man looked abashed but came forward, extending a large hand. He was a man of seventy or more, wide-shouldered and strong, with a head of wiry grey hair and long hairs, also grey, sprouting from between the buttons of his flannel shirt. He seated himself at the table, and when the kettle was ready she poured tea.

'You've told 'im then,' the man said. He seemed embarrassed to be addressing her in another man's presence.

'Yes, I told 'im. Not the whole of it, but.'

He nodded, sipped, gave me another sidelong glance. He was oddly defensive for so large a man. As if he saw in me a kind of power before which his strength would be of no account. Faced with whatever it was, he flinched, and his largeness, now that it had been dismissed, was like a burden to him. He seemed unhappy with his own shoulders and arms, handling the china cup with difficulty. But when the woman put her hand on his for a moment, and their eyes met, they seemed beyond any harm that I or anyone else might do them, inviolably contained in their own concern for one another.

His hairy Adam's apple worked up and down. He fisted his cup and drained it.

'Well,' he said, 'I'll be gettin' back.'

He got to his feet, and when he turned to go she called after him. 'Don't worry, George. It's oright, you know.'

He was framed for a moment in the light from the doorway. Sunlight was streaming down the hallway behind.

'If you say so, mother.'

He gave me a curt nod.

'I'll be back at five.'

She listened while he crossed the verandah and went on down the seven steps, and when she faced me again she had a look of command that I would not have predicted in so small a woman. She glowed; she rose to the heights of what she must have seen as her true self; and was imposing enough to convince me then that she might be just what she claimed to be, the daughter of one of the greatest performers of the age.

'Now,' she said, 'I'll tell you the whole story, and you will believe.'

IV

I should point out that the facts of the Diva's life, as I know from twenty years of attempting to follow her course from a South Coast dairy farm through half the capitals of the world, are so meagre as to be almost non-existent. A secretive woman, deeply suspicious of even her closest friends and advisers, she seems to have protected the truth about herself by spreading conflicting accounts of her parentage, her marriage, even of the place and date of her birth. It isn't that she lied exactly, any more than Bernhardt did. Rather, she allowed others to make suggestions, the wilder the better, and then herself added the flourishes. As the years wore on and she moved further from the source, the flourishes increased and predominated, grew more extravagantly baroque. The common truth, if it had been laid bare, would have had to be rejected. It no longer fitted her style.

In the early days, when she was just a prodigious voice that had appeared, almost miraculously it seemed, out of a far and empty land, she had let journalists tell people whatever they wanted to hear; to dream up previous lives for her that were appropriate to Odabella or Semiramis, since her own outlandish country was to her present admirers every bit as fantastic as theirs. So her father was said to be a nephew of Napoleon, who had settled in New South Wales in the Fifties and married a local heiress. Later her parents were *saltimbanques* in a travelling circus, Hungarian Jews, and she had been born on the Dunolly goldfields on the day the continent yielded up its most spectacular nugget, the 'Welcome Stranger'. Later again, when she was firmly established, she confessed (which again may not be true) that she came from a poor farming family near Bega and offered romantic views of herself wandering about the paddocks and singing as she brought in the cows. (A marvellously evocative image this: dusk in the green pastures above the surf, a barefoot girl sleep-walking through the gathering dusk as the first notes of that angelic voice touch the colonial air; to be heard, like some as yet undiscovered spirit of the landscape, by a stranger who pauses a moment on the road and wonders if he is dreaming, then shakes his head and goes on – her first obscure admirer, quite unaware of the grace he has been afforded.)

Evocative but unprovable. The versions of her past that are promulgated tend to mirror her current status. It is only late in life, when she had abandoned her more extravagant roles and become a household favourite, that the farmgirl appears.

Did she really marry at nineteen the keeper of a small-town hardware store, and pass bags of nails, and nuts and bolts and screws over the counter? What happened to the man? Why didn't he come forward in the days of her ascendancy to claim his bride? Did she pay him off? Did she hire bullies to scare him off? She was capable of it. Did he never realize that the great Vale and his sullen bride were one? When she makes her first appearance in the early Nineties she is in the company of an ageing tenor from an Italian touring group; but he too disappears and is just a name.

And in a way, of course, none of this matters. It is part of the legend that she exploded into the consciousness of an adoring public as a fully developed Voice, clothed in the jewels, the satin folds of a savage empress; that she came into existence as what she always endeavoured, after that, to remain: a dramatic illusion with no more past in the actual flesh than the characters she played. As well ask what Norma or Lucrezia Borgia were doing between seven and thirteen as imagine the Diva's childhood. Living legends are not born, brought up, schooled in this place or that. They burst upon us. They are spontaneously, mysteriously, inevitably, *there*.

It was always like that. Between seasons she simply disappeared; and though the rumours were many there were no facts.

Was she the mistress, the morganatic wife even, of the Comte de Paris? Did she marry and then abandon the Armenian munitions manufacturer? Her relationship with the court at St Petersburg was close enough for her to have had access to some of its most exclusive circles; but whether this was based on her quite unprecedented success in the theatre there or on some more personal tie cannot be confirmed. She destroyed the letters she received and herself wrote none – a few surviving notes are very nearly illiterate. Even her fortune cannot be traced. Terrified of being stranded without funds, she opened bank accounts in false names in some thirty or forty cities from Pittsburgh to Nanking, a good many of them still undiscovered and still accumulating interest, and when she died left no will.

Whether she herself believed the stories that circulated about her or was satisfied simply to be what she had become, the Earthly Angel, the Incomparable, la Vale, we shall never know. But there had been a childhood – parents and a home; there must even have been an original and quite ordinary name. She herself can't have forgotten. But they were her secret. What image she turned to when the costumes, the jewels, the bold lines of an Amelia or an Elisabetta were laid aside – that is the greatest of her mysteries. Who was she when she looked into her glass at five in the morning? Who was she in her sleep? (Imagine it, the Diva's sleep!) Inside the gestures of a dozen great characterizations, murderous queens and princesses, vengeful lovers, wronged maidens and other monsters, was a lost and secret child that only she could have recognized, and it was that child, grown into a sixty-year-old stranger, who came home at last and looks out at us, terrifying but also perhaps terrified by her own strangeness, in the photographs; a woman who has survived the life she created and is left now to resume the earlier, ordinary self she sailed away from and has never entirely outgrown.

So Mrs Judge's story, improbable as it might be, was not irreconcilable with the known facts. No story could be. Nor was it too wild to be believed. I listened in a dream. When she had finished, and we heard the man's step on the verandah, it was already dark. She gave a great sigh and leaned back, exhausted by the telling or the living of it – her own life, and seemed so touched for a moment with the grandeur and remoteness of tragedy, that I felt that if I so much as addressed her she might disintegrate like a being from another world. Better to get up and leave as one leaves a theatre, with the illusion still glowingly intact.

'You haven' lit the lamp,' the man said, looming in the doorway, surprised to find us in the dark.

She started then, and made a move.

'No, I'll do it,' he said. 'You sit and finish your talk.'

'We're finished,' she said, staring trancelike before her. 'We're almost finished.'

He moved about, pumping and lighting the lamp, and by the time he was done, and had set it on the table, she was once again the small, tired woman who had begun her story all those hours ago. She looked at her gnarled hands, then upward and met his gaze. She gave a soft smile.

'Don't worry, I'm oright. I'll see about gettin' yer tea in a minute. There's some corned beef.'

She got up heavily and went to the meat safe.

I declined her invitation to stay. The moment of communion between us had passed. The man's presence, and the sound of him washing now in a tin basin at the back, snuffling noisily as he splashed, put a kind of restraint upon her. She no longer belonged entirely to herself. She saw me out to the verandah steps.

It was still light outside. Palm-tops and bananas stood in silhouette against the sky and high overhead was a fast-moving cloud, a flock of what I took to be birds. It was the flying-foxes, making their way from the rain-forests further north to their feeding place on the other side of town. Millions of them. Having unfolded themselves out of the darkness under the boughs of trees, they were flying, now that the light was almost gone, in a dense and flickering cloud that might have been the coming of the dark itself. The sky was black with them.

On the top step of the verandah, set out like an offering, was a covered saucer, with beside it a frangipani; on the second step another. She leaned down and took them up, one in each hand, the rival offerings.

'My Indians,' she said smiling, and stood holding them up for me to see. More visible proof. There was a moment's pause while she let it sink in. 'So then,' she said, 'what will it mean?'

I didn't know. What could it mean, sixty years after the event, thirty years after the main character was dead? – No, that was wrong. *She* was the main character.

'I don't know,' I told her, a little alarmed by the possibilities, and not only for her. 'We'll have to see.'

She nodded.

'You know,' she said, 'I'm trusting you with me life. 'is as well'.

She jerked her head towards the lighted hallway.

I went on down the steps.

'I wouldn' dawdle if I was you,' she called after me, suddenly practical. 'From the looks a' that sky I'd say we was in for a storm. It'll be a thumper.'

V

The woman's life. Incredible. But the details of it demand to be believed, and so, now that I have looked into her eyes, does she. She has a kind of grandeur, our Mrs Judge, and for all her lack of education, an intelligence that immediately imposes itself. But she *is* uneducated, and much of what she has told me, if it is not her own experience, can only have come to her through the most painstaking research. She has at her fingertips dates, cast-lists, the names of even the most obscure of the Diva's colleagues and friends.

The local chemist, who knows all the history of Karingai, assures me that she has spent the whole of her life here, or the whole of his life anyway, and he is a man of fifty. She and her husband keep to themselves. They are visited only by her Indian neighbours and one or two related Indians from towns close by. For years now the other whites have avoided them. The rumour is that she is herself part-Indian and the man part-Aboriginal. After listening to her story I have come to the conclusion that the fairytale childhood she describes can only be her own.

Two of her memories especially impress me.

One is the story of her flight from St Petersburg to the Polish border in 1917, when she would have been ten.

She and her brother had been taken in their earliest infancy to Russia and were brought up there on the fringes of the court, the offspring, officially unrecognized, of a Grand Duke; so that as well as being the daughter of the Diva she is also, by her own account, a cousin of the Romanov children murdered at Ekaterinburg, and for that reason, she believes, still on the Bolshevik murder list. It was to escape their local agents that she took refuge, fifty years ago, at Karingai.

Of that earlier period she remembers almost nothing till the night of their flight over the snow: herself, her twin, and two ladies of high rank from the palace, all packed into a single sleigh.

Winter light, more glowingly blue than daylight, held the domes of the city in a dreamlike stasis as they made their way, closely covered against detection, over the Neva bridges and through the roaring streets; among carts, horses, peasants with swaying bundles, torches, confused cries and faces. Then, with the sleigh hissing and sighing on the hard-packed snow, out at last into a countryside that might have been laid under a spell: the birches crusted a sugary white, all sound damped and distanced – the old Russia of her childhood laid forever asleep in her head. Groups of stained wooden huts with alleys of ice-tipped mud between; tea fuming in cups, and strips of charred pork that grimed and burnt the fingers; forests, rivers of ice, a long swooning into an immensity of white where the days fell endlessly without sound and their passing left no track.

Later, towards the west, lines of grey-coated, grey-faced soldiers, some with their feet in rags, many of them maimed and bandaged, who turned out of half-sleep to watch their sleigh recede into the distance, as they turned in their own dream to watch the grey lines dwindle behind. A whiteness at last without detail; which is amnesia, oblivion; a blankness in which the boy, the twin brother, strays and is lost in some town swarming with refugees, carried off in a contrary direction on the tide of Russians, Ruthenians, Letts, Poles, Jews that is pouring south, east, west out of the mouths of war.

The lost brother still haunts her dreams. Her male counterpart. That Other who would guarantee the truth of who she is.

She recalls their sleeping together in the same hammock, innocently fitted together, spoon-fashion, and sharing perhaps the same dream. Two blue moths are hovering over them, borne back and forth on the breeze. There is the scent of pennyroyal.

Sometimes over the years she has woken to that scent and to the slight motion sickness of the hammock, and has almost recalled what dream it was they were sharing that had later taken the shape of moths, and almost recaptured the feeling of completeness with which their bodies fitted together, their lovely congruence.

Catching sight of herself sometimes in a glass, she has had the odd sense of being no longer one; has seen the mirror's depths swim a moment and another figure come to its surface. She stands face to face with herself then, but in some different time and place; feeling her limbs harden, her chest grow flat, the hair coarsen on her upper lip, as a deeper voice fumbles for words in her throat, and in a language she no longer speaks. Her feeling then is of painful incompleteness, of someone unrecognized and lost now for nearly sixty years, who wears a semblance of her own face and gropes through her for a memory of that forgotten dream, their childhood; stopping dead perhaps on the platform of some Polish border-town where he might be an inspector of trains, and half-recalling, as the distant names are called over the station loud-speaker, the dazzle of a courtyard, and a monk's bearded face leaning over them, a holy breath falling on their brows as they sit wrapped for their journey; or further back still, a garden with bowls of porridge

cooling on wooden benches, lemons cut in segments, a deep reson-
ance as of bees in the honey-coloured light of a hexagonal dome;
his thought fluttering with hers in a scent of pennyroyal, but no
longer knowing, as she does, what it refers to, and if he did know,
or thought he knew, finding no one now to believe him.

Her second recollection, which has perhaps crystallized the first
and given it coherence, is of a garden that descends via a tunnel and
steps to a wide and dazzling harbour.

It is Sydney, 1920. She is thirteen. She has come to Australia, and
this she remembers perfectly, from India, having been spirited south
out of Poland into Transylvania, and from there, with the remains
of their party, to Turkey; then south again on the caravan routes.
Weeks of swaying across a landscape of blinding light, with nothing
to break the horizon but an occasional outcrop or the bristling
gun-barrels of a band of brigands. Then, one cool morning, India,
valley on valley falling among threads of smoky water, long sighs
of relief after the desert-places, and a ridge of mist-shrouded deodars.
On narrow paths among the rhododendrons, pilgrims approach to
the sound of bells.

What happened there is another story. After negotiations carried
on between her own women and some local dignitary she was
gathered into the rich, precocious life of a palace, betrothed, in a
ceremony she recalls only as involving elephants and a great many
fireworks, to a minor prince.

But destiny acted yet again to push her on. At barely twelve she
bore a child, a son. He was snatched away at the very moment of
his birth by a rival faction at court, and when she woke after a
drugged sleep it was to find in his place a little rag doll. The doll
too she has by her still. I knew that immediately, from the look in
her eyes when she spoke of it, a little gesture of her head towards
the door of the bedroom; but she did not produce it. It is, I know,
the deepest of all her secrets. I imagine her sitting alone in the house,
behind the lattice, in the evening cool, nursing it, crooning to it,
speaking its name. After so long the lost child still comes to her in
dreams that leave her whole body racked and torn. A small mouth
tugs at her breast. She recalls a pain that for long hours fills the

room, beats against the walls, then breaks and falls away, to become in the long years afterwards the same pain but no longer physical, a heart-wrenching emptiness. That child, if it survived, would be a man of sixty. They are almost contemporaries, she, her brother and the child. He is, perhaps, living the life of a common peasant, quite unaware of his origins, working, hard-handed, hollow-thighed, in the mud of a paddy-field, always at the edge of starvation; another part of her, like the twin brother, that she has lost contact with but which moves in a separate and parallel existence in her mind.

Once again she was spirited away. And in Bombay, far to the south, no longer a wife or mother, was called one warm evening, lugging her rag doll, to a room in one of the great hotels on the waterfront, where a lady wearing a great many jewels shed tears, drew the child to her spiky breast, and claimed her as her own child recovered.

One sees how the scene might have gone. The Diva in fact had played it before. In *Lucrezia*. Finding in herself, to her own surprise and the delight of her admirers, the lineaments of a new and unexpected passion: beyond carnality and the lust for power or vengeance, the great emotion – maternal love. It was one of her triumphs.

She must herself have felt the oddness of it, that meeting in Bombay: of life's coming at last to imitate art – or had the fictive scene already had the real child in view? granting that there was a child; drawing on that as the source of its extraordinary power – of the emotion created to fill a role being required now, and in some ampler and more convincing form, to take on life itself. Clearly, in the Diva's case, it could not. When the great scene was played out and they came down to dusty daily existence, the child must have been just another traveller in the Vale circus, that rag-bag of managers, dressers, advisers, lovers, gambling cronies and other hangers-on that moved with her from capital to capital for as long as she was on the road. The child might have been with her for a season or two (no need to specify on what basis) and then she was not.

So now, in the smoky light of a summer afternoon in Sydney, she is lying in a hammock slung between thick, flowering trees. A voice drifts through the open window of the house above. *Batti, batti,* it is singing while someone plays the piano, the unseen hands fluttering up and down the keyboard on effortless wings, and the voice also disembodied, of the air ungraspable. She is a child again. And found.

Lying alone here, half-dozing in her white party dress, she gazes through flickering lids and an archway of stone to where the harbour, in a film of blue, gently rises and falls like the skin of some strange and beautiful animal that has come to sprawl at her feet, and whose breath she feels tugging the silk of her sleeves. The garden is full of scents: bruised gardenia, cypress, the ooze of gum. Insects are brooding over a damp place in the bushes where something is coming into existence, or has just left it. Clouds are building to a storm. Suddenly, up the long steps from the water, through the light of the archway, disguised now as a sailor and with his eyes burning in a wilderness of hair, his beard electrically alive, comes the monk Rasputin with a finger to his lips.

She knows him immediately. He reassures her of who she is and of where they have both come from. He too has escaped, lived through seven bullet-wounds in a frozen courtyard, after the murderers, terrified of his advance towards them – a mad dog dancing in the snow, that had already eaten poison and taken seven rounds of lead into his body – had turned on their heels and fled. Now he too is moving unrecognized through the world, waiting only to declare himself.

He has enemies and is pursued. He stays only long enough to warn her that she too has pursuers. When a voice calls from the house above he is startled, kisses the child's brow, raises his rough hand over her in a last blessing, and slips away in his sailor's garb down the long stairs to the water, where he pauses a moment and is framed against the stormy light, then descends to a waiting dinghy. Only the dark smell of his beard, which stirs her memory and is unmistakable, still remains with her. And it is this that she uses to evoke him, her one protector: his gnarled feet – the feet of a monk – retreating over the stone flags. And the water rhythmically lifting and falling, the breath of a drowsing beast . . .

Sixty years ago.

The voice calling from the terrace, having come to earth again, is her mother's. Alicia Vale.

VI

I was writing up the report of my Karingai lecture, comfortably at ease in dressing-gown and slippers, with a bottle of whisky at my elbow.

These things write themselves. Comfortable clichés, small white lies to convince the holders of the country's purse-strings that big things are being achieved out there in the wilderness, that we missionaries of the Arts are making daily converts to the joys of the spirit and to higher truth. I'm a whizz at such stuff. Devoting myself for half an hour to the official lie was a way of not facing my own difficult decision: how far I was prepared (Oh Adrian, not another of your discoveries! Yes, yes, my dears, Uncle Adrian's at it again!) to risk my reputation and face a cruelly sceptical world in defence of Mrs Judge's problematical birth.

The rain had come down as the woman predicted. Sheets of it! The earth turned to mud, bushes thrashed, trees swam in subaqueous gloom, the din on the roof of my motel cabin was deafening. So that I did not hear the tapping at first, and was startled when I glanced up out of the pool of lamplight to see framed in the dark of the window, and wordlessly signalling, like a man going down for the third time, the woman's husband, George. I hurried to the door to let him in but he refused to come further than the verandah. He stood there barefoot, his waterproof streaming.

'I ius' slipped out,' he told me, 'while she's sleeping. I wanted t' tell you a few things.' He set his lamp down on the boards.

'But you must come in,' I said. 'Come in and have a drink.'

He shook his head.

'No,' he said very solemnly. 'No I won't, if it's all the same.' He looked past me into the lighted room with its twin chenille bedspreads, its TV set, the hinged desk-lamp. 'I'm too muddy.'

He was, but I guessed there was another and deeper reason. It represented too clearly, that room, the world I had come from, a world of slick surfaces and streamlining, of appliances, of power, that threatened him, as it threatened the woman too at the very moment of her reaching out for it.

'I'll stay out 'ere, if you don't mind.'

So our conversation took place with the rain cascading from the guttering just a few feet away and in such a roaring that he could barely be heard.

He began to unbutton his cape. 'I jus' wanted,' he repeated, 't' tell you a few things.' He paused, his thumb and forefinger dealing awkwardly with a stud.

'Like – like them people she thinks 'ave been makin' enquiries about 'er. Over the years like. Well, I made 'em up.' He looked powerfully ashamed, standing barefoot with the streaming cape on his shoulders and his brow in a furrow. 'I wanted t' tell you that right off like. T' get things straight.' He met my eyes and did not look away. I turned up the collar of my gown, though it wasn't at all cold, and nodded; an inadequate representative, if that is what he needed, of the forces of truth. In other circumstances I might have got out of my embarrassment by doing a little dance. But he wasn't the man for that sort of thing, and at that moment I wasn't either.

'Y' see,' he said, 'I didn' want t' lose 'er. I didn' intend no harm. I wanted 'er t' think she needed me. I don't reckon it'll make all that much difference, will it? I mean, you'll still do what she wants.'

'I don't know. I don't *know* what she wants.'

'Oh, she wants people t' know at last. Who she *is*.' He shook his head at some further view of his own that he did not articulate, though he wrestled with it. 'I suppose it means she'll go back, eh? To them others.'

Which others? Who could he mean? Who did he think was out there – out *where*? – that she could go back to? Didn't he realise that sixty years had slipped by, in which day by day a quite different story had been unfolding, in the papers and out of them, that involved millions and was still not finished and held us all in its powerful suspense?

He began to button the cape again, which was easier to deal with than silence; then said firmly: 'I'm a truthful man for the most part, I reckon I can claim that. On'y – I didn't want t' lose 'er. She's a wonderful woman. You don't know! We've been happy together, even she'd say that. I tried t' make 'er happy and I've been happy meself. No regrets, no regrets at all! There hasn' been a cross word between us in all the years. That ought t' count for somethin'. When I first met 'er, y' know, she was just a girl – that light and small I was scared of even brushin' against 'er. I was a carter then, and she was workin' f' rich people, out at Vaucluse. We used t' talk after work, and one night she told me the whole thing. I never knew such a world existed. She wanted t' get away where they wouldn' be on to 'er, so we just kep' movin' till we holed up here.' He looked again, with a furrowing of his brow, at his own view of the thing. 'I better be gettin' back,' he said, 'before she wakes up an' starts worryin' where I am. She does worry, y' know. She was sleepin' when I left. Knocked out.' There was another silence. Then he put his hand out, as he had earlier in the day, and we shook.

'You do believe 'er, don't you?' he said, holding my hand in his giant grasp. 'It'd be best if you did, whatever it costs. She wants t' be known at last. But it's up to you. You just do whatever you reckon is the right thing. For all concerned.'

He broke his grip, took up the hurricane-lamp, and with a curt little nod went down into the rain, leaning heavily into the wall of it, and I watched the light, and the play of it on his cape, till it flickered out among the trees. Holding my dressing-gown about me, though it wasn't at all cold, I turned towards the empty room, its welcoming light and warmth, and was unwilling for a moment to go in. The sky roared, the big trees rocked and swayed, the water came sluicing down. The truth is that I have a great fear these days of being alone.

But this is Mrs Judge's story, not mine – or it is the man's. He after all was the first of her believers, and has spent fifty years keeping faith with his convictions and translating them, even in minor dishonesty, into the dailyness of living. Of everything I had heard it was this that most touched me: the vision of what a man might, after all, make of his life in the way of ordinary but honourable commitment, and the plainness with which he might present himself and say, *This is what I have given my life to. This is what I am.* If I hadn't been convinced by the woman's claim, her passionate certainty that she was something other than what she seemed, I must have been by his steadier one that he was, even in her shadow, himself.

Compared with his part in all this my own is trivial. I am the messenger, the narrator; and if the narrator too needs to be convinced of the truth of what he is telling, it isn't the same as laying his life down and presenting that as the measure of his belief. The scepticism of my colleagues, a flicker of irony on the lips of even the most straight-faced listener – that is all I will have to bear. I see already how the improbable side of my nature (how does a man become improbable, even to himself?) will immediately declare itself as with a twitch of an imaginary cloak I clap my hands, flourish my fingers in the air, and present out of my own longing for the extraordinary (that is how they will put it) a small, dark, barefoot woman in floral, the daughter of Alicia Vale. 'But she was perfect!' (They will be telling the story to others now, in a crowded bar, or over lobster shells at a business lunch, embellishing a little as all story-tellers do.) 'She couldn't have been more appropriate if he'd invented her. But then he did, didn't he? He must have!'

Oh yes, she is appropriate all right, our Mrs Judge. Too appropriate. She puts me to the test – not of belief but of the courage to come out at last from behind my clown's make-up, my simpering and sliding and dancing on the spot, to tell her story and give myself away.

The stories we tell betray us, they become our own. We go on living in them, we go on living outside them. The Bloody Sergeant comes on, announces that a battle has been won, bleeds a little, and after twenty rugged lines retires into oblivion. But what he has been called upon to tell has to be lived with and carried through a lifetime, out there in the dark. His own end comes later and is another story. Which another man must tell.

A MEDIUM

When I was eleven I took violin lessons once a week from a Miss Katie McIntyre, always so called to distinguish her from Miss Pearl, her sister, who taught piano and accompanied us at exams.

Miss Katie had a big sunny studio in a building in the city, which was occupied below by dentists, paper suppliers and cheap photographers. It was on the fourth floor, and was approached by an old-fashioned cage lift that swayed precariously as it rose (beyond the smell of chemical fluid and an occasional whiff of gas) to the purer atmosphere Miss Katie shared with the only other occupant of the higher reaches, Miss E. Sampson, Spiritualist.

I knew about Miss Sampson from gossip I had heard among my mother's friends; and sometimes, if I was early, I would find myself riding up with her, the two of us standing firm on our feet while the dark cage wobbled.

The daughter of a well-known doctor, an anaesthetist, she had gone to Clayfield College, been clever, popular, a good sport. But then her gift appeared – that is how my mother's friends put it, just declared itself out of the blue, without in any way changing her cleverness or good humour.

She tried at first to deny it: she went to the university and studied Greek. But it had its own end in view and would not be trifled with. It laid its hand on her, made its claim, and set my mother's friends to wondering; not about Emily Sampson, but about themselves. They began to avoid her, and then later, years later, to seek her out.

Her contact, it seemed, was an Indian, whose male voice croaked from the delicate throat about the fichu of coffee-dipped lace. But she sometimes spoke as well with the voices of the dead: little girls who had succumbed to diphtheria or blood poisoning or had been strangled in suburban parks, soldiers killed in one of the wars, drowned sailors, lost sons and brothers, husbands felled beside their dahlias at the bottom of the yard. Hugging my violin case, I pushed hard against the bars to make room for the presences she might have brought in with her.

She was by then a woman of forty-nine or fifty – small, straight, business-like, in a tailored suit and with her hair cut in a silver helmet. She sucked Bonnington's Irish Moss for her voice (I could smell them) and advertised in the *Courier Mail* under Services, along with Chiropractor and Colonic Irrigation. It was odd to see her name listed so boldly, E. Sampson, Spiritualist, in the foyer beside the lifts, among the dentists and their letters, the registered firms, Pty Ltd, and my own Miss McIntyre, LTCL, AMEB. Miss Sampson's profession, so nakedly asserted, appeared to speak for itself, with no qualification. She was herself the proof. It was this, I think, that put me in awe of her.

It seemed appropriate, in those days, that music should be separated from the more mundane business that was being carried on below – the whizzing of dentist's drills, the plugging of cavities with amalgam or gold, and the making of passport photos for people going overseas. But I thought of Miss Sampson, for all her sensible shoes, as a kind of quack, and was sorry that Miss Katie and the Arts should be associated with her, and with the troops of subdued, sad-eyed women (they were mostly women) who made the pilgrimage to her room and shared the last stages of the lift with us: women whose husbands might have been bank managers – wearing smart hats and gloves and tilting their chins a little in defiance of their having at last 'come to it'; other women in dumpy florals, with freckled arms and too much talc, who worked in hospital kitchens or cleaned offices or took in washing, all decently gloved and hatted now, but looking scared of the company they were in and the heights to which the lift wobbled as they clung to the bars. The various groups hung apart, using their elbows in a ladylike way, but using them, and producing genteel formulas such as 'Pardon' or 'I'm so sorry' when the crush brought them close. Though touched already by a hush of shared anticipation, they had not yet accepted their commonality. There were distinctions to be observed, even here.

On such occasions the lift, loaded to capacity, made heavy work of it. And it wasn't, I thought, simply the weight of bodies (eight persons only, a notice warned) that made the old mechanism grind in its shaft, but the weight of all that sorrow, all that hopelessness and last hope, all that dignity in the privacy of grief, and silence broken only by an occasional 'Now don't you upset yourself, pet,' or a whispered, 'George would want it, I know he would.' We ascended slowly.

I found it preferable on the whole to arrive early and ride up fast, and in silence, with Miss Sampson herself.

Sometimes, in the way of idle curiosity (if such a motive could be ascribed to her) she would let her eyes for a moment rest on *me*, and I wondered hotly what she might be seeing beyond a plump eleven-year-old with scarred knees clutching at Mozart. Like most boys of that age I had much to conceal.

But she appeared to be looking at me, not through me. She smiled, I responded, and clearing my throat to find a voice, would say in a well-brought-up, Little Lord Fauntleroy manner that I hoped might fool her and leave me alone with my secrets, 'Good afternoon, Miss Sampson.'

Her own voice was as unremarkable as an aunt's: 'Good afternoon, dear.'

All the more alarming then, as I sat waiting on one of the cane-bottomed chairs in the corridor, while Ben Steinberg, Miss McIntyre's star pupil, played the Max Bruch, to hear the same voice oddly transmuted. Resonating above the slight swishing and breathing of her congregation, all those women in gloves, hats, fur-pieces, packed in among ghostly pampas-grass, it had stepped down a tone – no, several – and came from another continent. I felt a shiver go up my spine. It was the Indian, speaking through her out of another existence.

Standing at an angle to the half-open door, I caught only a segment of the scene. In the glow of candlelight off bronze, at three-thirty in the afternoon, when the city outside lay sweltering in the glare of a blue-black thundercloud, a being I could no longer think of as the woman in the lift, with her sensible shoes and her well-cut navy suit, was seated cross-legged among cushions, eyes closed, head rolled back with all the throat exposed as for a knife stroke.

A low humming filled the room. The faint luminescence of the pampas-grass was angelic, and I was reminded of something I had seen once from the window of a railway carriage as my train sat steaming on the line: three old men – tramps they might have been – in a luminous huddle behind the glass of a waiting-shed, their grey heads aureoled with fog and the closed space aglow with their breathing like a jar full of fireflies. The vision haunted me. It was entirely real – I mean the tramps were real enough, you might have smelled them if you'd got close – but the way I had seen them changed that reality, made me so impressionably aware that I could recall details I could not possibly have seen at that distance or with the naked eye: the greenish-grey of one old man's hair where it fell in locks over his shoulder, the grime of a hand bringing out all its wrinkles, the ring of dirt round a shirt collar. Looking through into Miss Sampson's room was like that. I saw too much. I felt light-headed and began to sweat.

A flutter of excitement passed over the scene. A new presence had entered the room. It took the form of a child's voice, treble and whining, and one of the women gave a cry that was immediately supported by a buzz of other voices. The treble one, stronger now, cut through them. Miss Sampson was swaying like a flower on its stalk . . .

Minutes later, behind the door of Miss Katie's sunny studio, having shown off my scales, my arpeggios, my three pieces, I stood with my back to the piano (facing the wall behind which so much emotion was contained) while Miss Katie played intervals and I named them, or struck chords and I named those. It wasn't difficult. It was simple mathematics and I had an ear, though the chords might also in other contexts, and in ways that were not explicable, move you to tears.

There is no story, no set of events that leads anywhere or proves anything – no middle, no end. Just a glimpse through a half-open door, voices seen not heard, vibrations sensed through a wall while the trained ear strains, not to hear what is passing in the next room, but to measure the chords – precise, fixed, nameable as diminished fifths or Neapolitan sixths, but also at moments approaching tears – that are being struck out on an iron-framed upright; and the voice that names them your own.